Search for the SHADOWMAN

Joan Lowery Nixon

A YEARLING BOOK

Published by
Bantam Doubleday Dell Books for Young Readers
a division of
Bantam Doubleday Dell Publishing Group, Inc.
1540 Broadway
New York, New York 10036

The trademarks Yearling® and Dell® are registered in the U.S. Patent and
Trademark Office and in other countries.

ISBN: 0-440-41128-9

Reprinted by arrangement with Delacorte Press

Printed in the United States of America

September 1997 (book club edition)

20 19 18 17 16 15 14 13 12

For my grandson,
Andrew Thomas Quinlan,
with love

The Bonner Family Tree

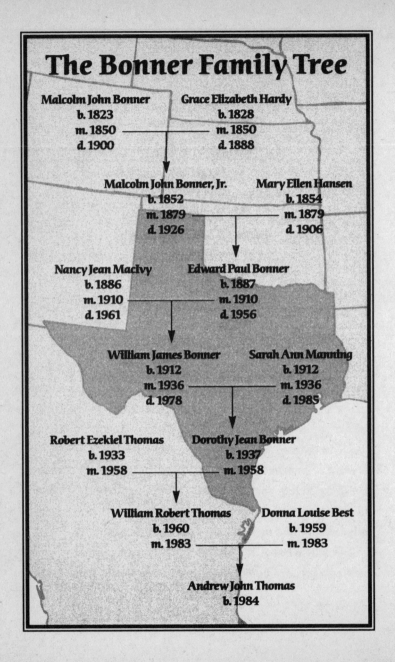

Malcolm John Bonner
b. 1823
m. 1850
d. 1900

Grace Elizabeth Hardy
b. 1828
m. 1850
d. 1888

Malcolm John Bonner, Jr.
b. 1852
m. 1879
d. 1926

Mary Ellen Hansen
b. 1854
m. 1879
d. 1906

Nancy Jean MacIvy
b. 1886
m. 1910
d. 1961

Edward Paul Bonner
b. 1887
m. 1910
d. 1956

William James Bonner
b. 1912
m. 1936
d. 1978

Sarah Ann Manning
b. 1912
m. 1936
d. 1985

Robert Ezekiel Thomas
b. 1933
m. 1958

Dorothy Jean Bonner
b. 1937
m. 1958

William Robert Thomas
b. 1960
m. 1983

Donna Louise Best
b. 1959
m. 1983

Andrew John Thomas
b. 1984

CHAPTER ONE

"Why'd Mr. Hammergren give us such a dumb assignment?" Andy Thomas complained to his best friend, J.J. Andy impatiently kicked at a small rock. It skittered across the street, dust swirls rising in its wake. "Why can't we study something important? Like outer space? What if a comet comes smashing toward Earth while we're busy asking our relatives about what life was like when they were kids? Who cares?"

As J.J. brushed a strand of light brown hair from his eyes, he tried to be patient with his friend. "We're studying Texas *history,* noodle brain. History means what happened in the past, not the future."

"Texas history! It's just a bunch of wars, cattle drives, and outlaws." *Outlaws?* "Hey, that's good! What if our relatives weren't just ordinary? What if they were bandits and train robbers?"

J.J. didn't answer.

"I mean it," Andy said, beginning to enjoy his own idea of being related to a Western desperado who rode with a holster low on his hips.

"Sure," J.J. finally answered. "I can just see my great-grandma Minna on a horse, waving smoking six-shooters. Or your great-aunt Winnie."

Both Andy and J.J. bent over, shouting with laughter at the thought of their very proper relatives—elderly ladies of more than ninety—hooting and hollering down the main street of Hermosa.

When Andy was finally able to talk, he said, "You've got it easy, J.J. Your great-grandma's done all that genealogy stuff. Your family has been naming their kids after the first James Jonathan Gasper forever. I forget, what are you, J.J., the fifth or sixth?"

"Seventh."

As they reached the driveway to the Gasper family's imposing white brick house with its impressive row of Ionic columns across the long front veranda, Andy teased, "Maybe I should interview Miz Minna, too. She's been around so long she could tell us almost everything there is to know about every family in Hermosa."

Instead of laughing, J.J. looked uncomfortable. "I know what people say about her gossiping, and they're right. She wouldn't be any help with your family's stories."

"I was just kidding," Andy said, worried that he had hurt his friend. "Miss Winnie's stories are going to be all I can handle. I've heard over and over about how it was before electricity came to West Texas, and about one-room schools and spelling bees and taffy pulls instead of television and video games. Now, because of Mr. Hammergren, the king of seventh-grade history, I've got to listen to it all over again."

"Not just listen, write it down and get a grade!" J.J. reminded him. He laughed and ran toward his porch.

Write it down. Sure, thought Andy. *As if I haven't got anything better to do.*

He headed toward home—a comfortable one-story brick house on a street two blocks from the Gaspers'. His family lived next door to his dad's parents and Miss Winnie. She had left the family ranch and had come to live next door when Andy was only seven years old.

Andy pictured Miss Winnie and Miz Minna again and chuckled—not at the notion of the two elegant old ladies as part of the Wild West, but at the stuck-up, snippy rivalry that existed between them.

Neither Miss Winnie Bell Bonner nor Miz Minna Gasper would miss a party, the opening night of a play at the Hermosa Community Theater, or the visiting symphony orchestra that performed in the high-school auditorium each fall and spring. They were often in the same group. But their words to each other were as brittle and cold as ice splinters.

Once when Andy had asked his mother what caused Miss Winnie and Miz Minna to be like that, she'd answered, "Some old feud, I suppose. It's gone on for so long, I wouldn't be surprised if neither of them remembers what started it. I certainly don't!"

When he'd asked J.J. if he knew, J.J.'s glance had slid to one side, and his face had turned red with embarrassment. "Miz Minna's kind of stuck-up," he'd said, "and my mom says she's too quick to say what she thinks. Whatever happened between them was probably Miz Minna's fault."

Five years ago, when J.J. and Andy had become best friends, J.J. had introduced Andy to Miz Minna, a short, plump woman with a face like a soft, pink-tinted marshmallow.

In her high, sugary voice, Miz Minna had settled herself into a high-backed, overstuffed chair and said, "So you're Andrew Thomas. Turn around, child. Let me get a good look at you."

Awkward and uncomfortable, Andy felt as if he had to follow her order.

When he had faced her again, Miz Minna had pursed her lips, continued to study him, and said, "Hmmm. Dark, curly hair, blue eyes, a little on the stocky side. You do look like a Thomas."

Andy had laughed. "I *am* a Thomas."

Her eyes opened wide, she blinked twice, and the sweetness slid from her voice like syrup down the drain. "Don't get uppity. Unfortunately, I can see some of the Bonner blood in you too, young man."

Puzzled, Andy began, "Miss Winnie is a Bonner, and my grandma Dorothy, so my dad—"

Miz Minna interrupted. She reached out to ruffle J.J.'s hair and said quickly, "Run along, y'all. Don't make too much noise, don't break anything, and don't get into trouble."

As soon as they'd left the room, J.J. had grinned and said, "Don't mind Miz Minna. She orders me around like that all the time."

Andy was glad that J.J. wasn't as stuck-up as his great-grandmother. He guessed if anybody had a right to be conceited, it was J.J. The library, the bank, the high school, Hermosa's largest department store, and even the fountain in the park were named after the original James Jonathan Gasper, one of the men who had helped build the town of Hermosa. Gasper's bronze statue stood tall and dignified in front of the court-house. Even under a crown of pigeon droppings it looked impressive.

As Andy ran up the driveway to his back door, he wished once more that his class could have left the past behind and written instead about the future. The future was exciting, especially outer space, but the past?

He sighed, knowing he didn't have a choice. He

5

wanted a good grade, so he'd better interview Miss Winnie and get his paper written.

Andy gulped down a glass of milk and two chocolate brownies before he left a note for his mom on the refrigerator. He wanted her to find it as soon as she got home from her job at the bank. He grabbed a notebook and pencil and ran next door to visit his great-aunt, crunching through the dried cottonwood and elm leaves that dusted the lawn.

His slender, blond grandmother, Dorothy Thomas, led him into the parlor, cool and dim with the drapes drawn against the afternoon sun. The room smelled tangy with lemon oil from the highly polished tables, and a light fragrance of cinnamon drifted in from the kitchen.

Grandma Dorothy gave Andy a hug. "You're out of breath. What's the rush?" she asked.

"Homework," Andy said. "We've got to write a history of our family. I'm supposed to start by interviewing the oldest member available." As he glanced toward the glassed-in back porch, where Miss Winnie liked to read and knit, he lowered his voice. "She always tells the same old stories."

"If you want new stories, ask her some new questions," Grandma Dorothy said.

"What new questions?"

"That's up to you."

Andy looked at his grandmother with hope. "Hey,

Grandma," he said, "you're kind of old. Maybe I could skip Miss Winnie and interview you."

Grandma rolled her eyes and put her hands on her hips. "Now my dear, stick to Plan A. Talk to Miss Winnie first. Then you can interview the rest of us decrepit old folks."

"What I meant," Andy said, but his grandma was already on her way to the kitchen. Bracing himself, he walked to the sunlit back porch, with its wicker rockers, potted plants, and countless embroidered pillows, and greeted his great-aunt Winnie Bell Bonner. Today he looked at her and saw a tiny woman with tightly curled white hair and smile-line crinkles at the corners of her mouth and eyes.

As Andy settled on the footstool next to Miss Winnie's rocking chair, he explained the interviews he had to do.

Even before he'd finished, Miss Winnie's eyes sparked with indignation. "I don't know why this Mr. Hammerhead's got an interest in other folks' family business."

"Hammergren. I don't think he's being nosy, Miss Winnie," Andy said. "He wants us to write the oral histories of our families so the old stories won't be lost."

"Some of those old stories are better off being lost and long forgotten," she snapped.

"But you've been telling us stories for years about

taffy pulls and what kinds of things you ate and the clothes you wore and all that stuff. You want those to be lost and forgotten?"

Miss Winnie hunched over, leaning forward, so that her nose was close to Andy's. She smelled faintly of the dried rose petals Grandma Dorothy kept in bowls in the bedrooms.

"Everybody knows about trifling things like clothes and taffy pulls," Miss Winnie said. "It's the *people* stories your teacher wants. It's the *people* stories that make history."

"Okay," Andy said. He opened his notebook and held up his pencil. "Tell me some *people* stories."

Miss Winnie thought a moment. "Some stories are for the telling, some are not," she said. "I'll decide which are which."

"Why should some stories not be told?" Andy asked. Suddenly he was curious. Really curious.

"Never you mind." Miss Winnie shook her head.

Andy shrugged. "Okay, then," he said, "I guess I should ask you some of the questions Mr. Hammergren had us copy off the board. They're about transportation and how you handled sandstorms and how work was done in the home and stuff like that. They're not exactly people stories. I don't know where else to start."

Miss Winnie leaned back and waved a hand, shooing away the questions like flies. "I'll begin back as far as I heard tell, when in 1879 the Bonner family came to

8

West Texas to live. You've got a pencil, Andy boy. I'll start talking and you start writing."

"I'm ready, Miss Winnie," Andy answered, grinning. He remembered his conversation with J.J. "By the way, if there's any bank robbers or horse thieves in the family, don't forget to include them."

Miss Winnie's spidery-veined hands flew up to her cheeks. In a quavery voice she asked, "What have you heard? Just who've you been talking to?"

She looked so pale that Andy was scared. "Nobody! I was just teasing, Miss Winnie. Honest," he said.

Miss Winnie rested her head against the back of the rocker, closed her eyes, and took three long, deep breaths. The pink came back to her cheeks, and her eyes opened as she answered, "I was, too. Now, let's start with my great-grandfather, Malcolm John Bonner."

CHAPTER
TWO

Under Miss Winnie's eagle eye, Andy dutifully wrote down almost every word she said. Malcolm John Bonner may have brought his wife and near-grown children to settle in Hermosa at great personal sacrifice, but Andy found it hard to really care.

Now part of his mind was on his great-aunt's strange reaction to his comment about horse thieves and bank robbers. She'd said she'd tell him only those stories she wanted to tell. Was she hiding something?

Miss Winnie took a deep breath. "Now that we've got the begats out of the way, we'll—"

"The what?" Andy interrupted.

"The begats. You know. Malcolm John and his wife, Grace Elizabeth, begat Malcolm John Bonner, Jr., who married Mary Ellen Hansen, who begat . . ." She shrugged impatiently and reached up to tug a small embroidered pillow to a spot behind her left shoulder. "You wrote it all down. I watched you. Let's start with Malcolm John's story."

"Yes, ma'am," Andy said.

"Malcolm John Bonner brought his family to West Texas in terrible poverty," Miss Winnie began.

"Why'd they have to move? Especially if they were so poor?" Andy asked.

"They had no choice." Miss Winnie shook her head sadly, but her glance at Andy was wary. "Grace Elizabeth was sickly in the damp, humid climate of Corpus Christi, where they lived. Their doctor said the only way she'd survive would be to move to a dry climate."

"But they had no money to move."

"I didn't say that," Miss Winnie insisted. "They were good, frugal people. Malcolm John Bonner built and ran a successful dry goods store. He sold it and bought ranch land here in Hermosa, where people were gathering because they'd heard the railroad was planning to come through. But the money he'd saved to build a house and buy stock . . . that was stolen. Every cent of it."

Andy stopped writing and stared at Miss Winnie. The story was beginning to get interesting. "Who stole the money?" he asked.

"That was long ago and best forgotten," she answered. She looked away from Andy and went on.

"Malcolm John and his sons worked mighty hard for anyone who could afford to pay for hired help. Grace Elizabeth and her daughters became seamstresses and milliners, and . . ."

Andy had barely opened his mouth before Miss Winnie said, "That means they made dresses and hats for other folk."

"Okay," Andy said, and wrote fast.

"As I was about to say," Miss Winnie told him, "the family worked hard, saved as much money as possible, and eventually were able to buy some livestock and develop their land."

"Good!" Andy exclaimed, surprised at the rush of relief he felt that these relatives from the past had come through their troubles.

Grandma Dorothy walked into the room and rested a hand on Miss Winnie's shoulder. "Andy, why don't you come back tomorrow afternoon?" she asked. "We're having an early supper so we can take in a movie."

He closed his notebook and stood up. "Thanks for your help, Miss Winnie. See you."

"Delighted," Miss Winnie answered. "In the meantime, if you want, go up to the attic and look for a large cardboard box with 'Winnie Bell Bonner' printed on it. When I moved here from the ranch, I crammed it full of family papers and photos. You might find something you can use for this school project."

"Great," Andy said, although he didn't mean it. Interviewing relatives and writing down what they said was going to take a lot of time. He edged toward the back door, but Grandma Dorothy stopped him. "This would be a good time to get the box, Andy. I know where it is. You'll find it on top of a trunk against the back wall of the attic."

It didn't take Andy long to find the box. It was heavy, but he balanced his notebook on top and managed to carry it down the stairs.

As he staggered through the back door of his own home, his mother, who had been looking through the day's mail, glanced up in surprise and rose to help him. Strands of reddish brown hair clung to her cheeks, her tailored blouse and skirt were wrinkled from the late September heat, and she had kicked her shoes off.

"Hello. What in the world is that?" she asked.

"I dunno," Andy said. "Miss Winnie said it was full of papers and photos that might help me with my genealogy report."

"I can't wait to see what's in here," she said, cutting the tape on the sealed box with the letter opener. "I'd love to know more about the Bonners."

"Then I wish you could write the report, instead of me!" Andy told her.

"Oh, come on, Andy," Mrs. Thomas said as she pulled off the top of the box. "This is fun. Let's take a look."

In spite of himself, he was intrigued as his mother gently removed a handful of papers, smoothing them against the kitchen tabletop and laying them flat. "Letters . . . a bill of sale for livestock . . . an old receipt for county property taxes . . . Oh! Here's a child's drawing," she said, then reached into the box for a framed photograph.

"My, my, look at this," she murmured. "You'll have to ask Miss Winnie who all these people are. It looks like a family portrait, taken at a party."

Andy, who could almost match his mother's height, leaned over her shoulder, studying the faded, brown-tinged, double row of unsmiling adults—so many they filled the photo, crowding against the narrow wooden frame. The women were dressed in high-necked, long-sleeved dresses, with skirts that touched the ground. The men's necks were squeezed uncomfortably inside stiff, high collars that poked above high-buttoned coats.

"It must have been a terrible party," Andy said. "They all look miserable."

"Back in the eighteen hundreds, people didn't usually smile when they had their photographs taken," his mother said. "For one thing, they had to hold still without moving for a long time, while the photo was being made. Also, many of them had missing teeth! Dental work wasn't what it is today."

Andy peered more closely. "The men are wearing

something around their necks," he said. "They look like bolo ties, except they each end in a circle."

"Like this?" His mother fished a narrow strip of leather from the box. Hanging from the middle of it was a horseshoe nail, hammered flat.

"Weird," Andy said as he took it and examined it. He hung it around his own neck.

Mrs. Thomas reached into the box again. "Oh, look, there are some books in here, too. What's this? A poetry book. And this one looks like a child's reader." She pulled out a thick, heavy book with a worn, frayed leather cover. "This must be an old family Bible," she said.

She opened it and held it toward Andy so that he could see a faded list of names. "Malcolm John Bonner," she said. "He wrote his birthdate and date of marriage to Grace Elizabeth Hardy. And their children are listed underneath." She touched the page lightly. "Someone has added their dates of death, as well. This is a real treasure."

"They sure had a lot of kids," Andy said. "There's a second Malcolm John Bonner, and an Elizabeth Anne, Margaret Jane, Cole Joseph, Peter James, Victoria Grace, and Rose Marie. Looks like for a while Mrs. Bonner had a baby every other year, or even closer."

"Back then people had big families because they knew they'd lose some of their children to illness," Mrs.

Thomas told Andy. "Look at the dates of birth and death. Victoria Grace and Rose Marie were infant deaths. Peter James lived only into his mid-twenties."

Andy stared at one name on the page. "I don't get it," he said. "Cole Joseph had a birthdate—August 1, 1856—but not a date of death, and somebody put a line through his name. Isn't that weird?"

His mother shrugged. "That's something to ask Miss Winnie about."

Andy took a step toward the back door as he said, "Grandpa, Grandma, and Miss Winnie are going to a movie, but I think I can catch them before they leave."

"When's the report due?" Mrs. Thomas asked.

"In a couple of weeks," Andy answered.

"Then visit Miss Winnie tomorrow. She'll tell you then." Mrs. Thomas smiled. "You're really interested in this project, aren't you?" she observed.

"I can make it," Andy insisted as he fingered the flattened nail. "I just have to ask her two questions." He was sure Miss Winnie had a secret, a family story she didn't want told, and he was beginning to suspect that the story had to do with Cole Joseph Bonner.

Andy ran through the crackling leaves, promising himself he'd rake them up for Grandpa as soon as he found time. He arrived just as Grandpa and Grandma were helping Miss Winnie down the back steps.

"Me again," he called. "I only want to ask you two questions, Miss Winnie!" Andy paused, gulping in a long breath. He held up the nail on the leather thong he was wearing. "What is this?"

Miss Winnie smiled. "That's a nail from the shoes of Malcolm John Bonner's horses. He made those circles for himself and his sons to wear. I believe they stood for his faith in the family's future. A circle means 'unbroken,' you know."

"They all wore them?"

"So I heard. Always."

Grandma Dorothy looked at her watch, so Andy quickly said, "The last question's about Malcolm John Bonner's family Bible."

Miss Winnie started. "The Bible? That was in the box?"

"All the names listed had birthdates as well as dates of death—all except one. Cole Joseph Bonner. Somebody drew a line through his name."

Miss Winnie leaned heavily on Grandpa Zeke's arm. "There was no Cole Joseph Bonner," she said so firmly that the tight white curls on her forehead bounced.

"His name was right there," Andy persisted. "It was written in the same handwriting as the other names. So sure there was. You know why it was crossed out? Please tell me."

"Listen to me, Andy boy," Miss Winnie said. "You're poking your nose into matters where it shouldn't be poked. I don't care what your Mr. Hammerhead assigned. Leave Coley Joe out of it. You're going to stir up problems that you and the family can't handle."

"Coley Joe? You called him Coley Joe! That means you know about him!"

Miss Winnie's finger waggled at Andy's nose. "Don't ask me questions about him, because you won't get any answers," she said. "As far as I'm concerned, he never existed. Forget all about Coley Joe, or you're going to cause all of us a great deal of trouble!"

CHAPTER THREE

That evening Andy had other homework to do. But he found time to call J.J., whom he told about Coley Joe.

"Maybe someone in our family really was a horse thief or a train robber," Andy said. "I wish I could find out."

"If Miss Winnie won't answer questions about him, why don't you just let it drop?"

"She didn't say I couldn't ask someone else."

"But you said she didn't want anyone to know about him because it would cause trouble," J.J. reminded him.

"I don't know what kind of trouble Coley Joe could cause. He was born in 1856. That's a long time ago." Andy paused and added, "J.J., I could see that my knowing about Coley Joe scared her."

"Then why don't you just do what she said?" J.J. asked. "Forget about him."

Andy fingered the leather thong he still wore around his neck. "I just can't."

When J.J. didn't respond to that, Andy said, "Listen, J.J., your family has an important great-great-great-great in it. Half the town's named after him. And you've got a cousin who's acted in two movies and an uncle who went to Washington as a congressman. Nobody in my family's done anything like that. The most exciting thing that's ever happened to anyone in the family was when Uncle Jeff, on my mom's side, won a trip to the Super Bowl. Don't you see? I *need* Coley Joe."

"What about your aunt Winnie?"

"I won't do anything that would hurt her. Whatever I find out about Coley Joe will be my secret. I think that's fair."

"Okay, I guess," J.J. said. "It's up to you."

"And maybe to you. Or your great-grandmother, that is."

"Miz Minna?"

"I'd like to talk to her. Just to ask if she ever heard of Coley Joe. Is that okay with you?"

"Are you sure you want to find out?" J.J. asked. "He may have done something you really don't want to know about."

Andy felt suddenly defensive. "Well, maybe he didn't."

"Then his name wouldn't have been crossed out."

Andy didn't like the way the conversation was going. "You watch too many old cowboy movies," he said.

"You're the one who said maybe he was a train robber or—"

Andy interrupted. "I'll see you tomorrow and stop off to visit Miz Minna when we walk home. Okay?"

As Andy hung up the phone he heard J.J. saying, "Okay . . . I guess."

The minute the bell rang in history class the next morning, Mr. Hammergren asked, "How many of you have begun your interviews with relatives?"

Lee Ann Dooley waved a hand. "I can't! My grandma in Florida just got married again and is off on a honeymoon. And my grandma who lives in a rest home can't remember much of anything."

"Then ask your parents if they've heard any of your grandparents' stories. Go back as far as you can. Maybe your family history will begin when your parents were children."

"Everyone else has grandparents." Lee Ann's lower lip curled outward. Her glance fixed on J.J. "Or even a *great*-grandparent."

"Tell you what," Mr. Hammergren said. "I'll let you borrow my grandmother. She won't know any stories about *your* family, but she can tell you about riding streetcars when she visited the big city and canning vegetables and making jam and sewing all the clothes for a family of six girls. See me after class and I'll give you her phone number if you'd like to speak to her."

He glanced around the classroom. "Anyone else having trouble getting started?"

Harvey Marks spoke up. "My great-grandpa has got some good stories about things he did with his cousins while he was growing up, but he can't keep their names straight."

"Did his cousins live in Hermosa?"

Harvey nodded.

"It won't be hard for you to get the right names," Mr. Hammergren said. "If they were born here, you can look for their birthdates in county records. If they died here, you can do the same." He smiled. "Or you might even go to the cemetery and check the names on the tombstones. Some of the old tombstones have information on them that isn't in the cemetery's records."

"But don't visit the cemetery at night," Nelson Banks growled in a scary voice, and everyone laughed.

Luke Martin raised his hand. "I've got a problem, Mr. Hammergren," he said. "When my mom's father was young, he got in a fight and went to jail. Mom said under no circumstances could I put that in my report."

"I certainly don't expect you to include every single family story you discover," Mr. Hammergren said. "Record the best. Make your report interesting. And remember that it's better to leave some things out of the report."

"Like the mystery man." Andy realized he had spoken aloud when some of the kids turned and looked at him.

"What mystery man?" Lee Ann asked.

Andy carefully gave his explanation. "He's one of my dad's relatives, from way back in the eighteen hundreds. His birthdate was listed in the family Bible, but then his name was crossed out. My great-aunt Winnie first said he never existed. Then she told me not to ask questions about him because she wouldn't answer them."

"Then I'd suggest you forget this mystery relative," Mr. Hammergren said. "This report is not intended to cause family problems."

But Andy's mind was on Coley Joe. He wasn't about to forget him.

Lila Martinez, the Gaspers' housekeeper, opened the door just as J.J. reached for the knob. She smiled and said, "Hey, J.J. Hey, Andy. How's it going?"

"Fine, Lila," J.J. answered.

"You came because you knew I just took some cookies out of the oven. Right, Andy?"

Andy smiled. "I came for cookies and homework. We're here to do some homework, Mrs. Martinez."

She cocked her head as though she were studying Andy, and her eyes twinkled. "That doesn't look like a homework face. It looks like you're up to something."

"We're doing research on our family histories," Andy said. "And we're going to see if Miz Minna will answer some of our questions."

Lila's smile grew broader. "She'll be glad for a little company. All her old lady friends were either at the beauty parlor, the doctor, or visiting relatives today, so Miz Minna's been bored with no one to talk to. She's in her sitting room. Please tell her I'll bring up cookies and something cold to drink in a couple of minutes."

Lila left, but J.J. hesitated at the foot of the stairs. "Why don't we forget the history homework for now and shoot baskets?" he asked.

"After the questions," Andy insisted. He marched around J.J. and up the stairs.

The door to Miz Minna's sitting room was wide open. In a dark blue silk dress, with the opera-length pearls she always wore, she sat framed against the wide, velvet-swagged window. In spite of the puffiness around her eyes and chin, Andy was reminded of the painting of a duchess he had seen on a field trip to the Dallas Museum of Art.

Miz Minna had been watching a television show, and

24

she quickly clicked off the power as Andy tapped on the door frame.

"Come in, boys," she called in her soft little sugar voice. "How nice of y'all to come and visit me. Does Lila know you're here?"

"She said to tell you she'd send up cookies and something cold to drink," J.J. answered. He bent to kiss Miz Minna's forehead.

Miz Minna beamed and said, "Sit down. Please, sit down. Pull those chairs a little closer, but don't break anything while you're doing it. Watch the vase, J.J."

"Yes, ma'am," J.J. answered politely.

"Did J.J. tell you that I'm making it easy for him to write his history report?" Miz Minna asked Andy. "Over the past few years, not only have I researched our genealogy by hunting in old family records, but I've bought books about the time periods. I have volumes that show the kinds of clothes people wore, what they used for cooking, the buggies and surreys they rode in. It makes me glad that there's a good deal of information J.J. can finally use."

J.J. looked embarrassed, but Andy simply asked, "How did you do all that research?"

"Some of it came from old family records, including a very special journal kept by the first James Jonathan Gasper, but most of it I did by computer." Miz Minna winked coyly. "The electronic age is not just for the younger generation."

Andy glanced at the computer and printer on a desk at the far side of the room. "Do you mean you used the computer to look up stuff about your family?"

"Not only that. If you enter the Internet directly or subscribe to a computer service, you can link into some of the world's finest genealogy centers, such as the Family History Library in Salt Lake City. And the bulletin boards are useful, too."

"Bulletin boards?"

Impatiently, J.J. said, "You know about computers, Andy. Miz Minna uses the place where people send messages to each other. In the genealogy boards they write messages asking for help in finding information about old guys who are supposed to be part of their family trees."

"J.J.!" Miz Minna snapped. "They are not 'old guys,' as you put it. I was able to trace our own branch of the family back to some highly respected gentlemen from the Carolinas." As her voice softened, she preened and said, "Why, the first James Jonathan Gasper's father, Wilfred Edmunton Gasper, fought as a major in the War Between the States.

Andy didn't think he'd better ask which side, but he thought that if Miss Winnie could learn to use his dad's computer, then she could look up her ancestors, too.

Lila Martinez brought in a tray of snacks.

"Miz Minna, you know just about everything about

everybody who ever came to Hermosa, don't you?" Andy asked.

She almost giggled and said modestly, "Well, I wouldn't exactly say that."

"Do you know anything about Coley Joe Bonner? He was born in 1856."

A smug smile crossed her lips. "Why are you asking about Coley Joe Bonner?"

"Because he's kind of a mystery man in our family. I found his name written in Malcolm John Bonner's family Bible, along with their other children, but his name was crossed out, and there wasn't a date of death."

"Did you ask Miss Winnie about him?"

"Miss Winnie said he didn't exist."

Miz Minna leaned forward. "Oh, he existed, all right, or his name and birthdate wouldn't have been written into the Bible."

"Then why was it crossed out?"

Miz Minna sighed plaintively. "On rare occasions— very rare, you understand—a son or daughter so disgraced the family that a father would cross out the name. It was a symbol that the person was no longer a part of the family."

Andy felt as though a rock had dropped into his stomach. Sure, he'd told J.J. that it would be fun to have a bank robber or horse thief in the family, but he realized he hadn't really meant it.

"Do you know what Coley Joe did to get crossed out of the family?" Andy asked.

"Yes, indeed. There's proof. However, it's not up to me to rattle other families' skeletons," Miz Minna said. "You'd better ask Miss Winnie to tell you."

Her eyes narrowed as she thought, and her voice shifted from sweet to salty. "On the other hand, maybe you'd better not," she warned him. "Sometimes asking too many questions leads to trouble."

CHAPTER FOUR

"Now what?" Andy asked, after he and J.J. had said goodbye to Miz Minna and walked out to the front porch. "She told me to talk to Miss Winnie, but Miss Winnie said if I asked her any questions about Coley Joe she wouldn't answer them."

"Leave him out of your report," J.J. said. "We don't have to write about all of our relatives. Mr. Hammergren said so. We're supposed to collect stories about how the older people in our family lived, way back when. Coley Joe Bonner has nothing to do with what Mr. Hammergren wants."

"It's weird. Miz Minna said if I asked questions I could cause trouble. That's the same thing Miss Winnie told me."

"Then don't ask questions. Forget about Coley Joe."

Andy looked up as he heard the exasperation in his best friend's voice. "It's just that to me Coley Joe is almost like a real person and . . ."

"He *was* a real person," J.J. said, "but no matter what he did or didn't do, he died a long time ago, and his problems are over. We've got a big test in math tomorrow. I don't know about you, but I've got to study for it."

"I'll see you in the morning," Andy said.

He walked home double time and unlocked the back door. There, still on one end of the kitchen table, rested Miss Winnie's box of family mementos. Andy dropped his backpack onto the nearest chair. He felt himself drawn to the box as surely as if someone were leading him toward it.

He reached into the box for the Bonner family Bible, eager to see the list of names one more time, but he discovered that the Bible was missing.

Grabbing the framed photograph, an old bankbook, and a fistful of papers, Andy shoved them onto the tabletop. He rummaged through the remaining items in the box with a terrible, scary feeling. Some of the papers his mom had put together were gone, too!

Andy groaned and flopped into a chair. It was then he noticed the sheet of note paper held to the refrigerator door with a magnet. He walked across the room, pulled the paper off, and read:

Andy,

I took the Bible and a few of the more interesting papers we found. I'll make copies of them and of the list of Bonner names for you to include with your report. I love you.

Mom

With a wave of relief Andy flopped back into his chair, but as he did so, his elbow struck the framed Bonner family photograph, knocking it from the table. He grabbed for it, but he was too late. With a thud, one corner of the frame hit the floor and split. Andy groaned as he heard the glass shatter.

In an instant he was on his knees, cautiously avoiding the shards of glass. He gently held up the splintered frame. In his fingers the old wood slid apart, dropping to the floor with the remaining glass. The photograph and its cardboard backing sailed under the table.

It wasn't until after Andy had carefully picked up all the pieces of wood and glass and put them into the wastepaper basket that he dared to crawl under the table and examine the photo. He could use his allowance to get the photograph reframed.

To Andy's relief, the photo itself didn't seem to be damaged. As he picked it up, however, he saw that one end of the photo had been curled back around the cardboard. He could see the shoulder of a man, a shoulder that had been covered by the frame.

31

He carefully flattened and smoothed the photo against the tabletop, revealing the smiling face of a young man—a young man who looked strangely familiar. Even though that portion of the photograph was dark and the man seemed to be standing in shadow, Andy could see that the smile, the eyes, and the dark curly hair were a lot like his own.

Andy gulped and sat up straight. "Who are you, shadowman?" Andy whispered.

Slowly he turned the photo over. In pencil someone had written the date, 1876, and the names of the people in the photograph behind where they had been standing in front of the camera. Andy held his breath, hoping, knowing what he would find: *Elizabeth Anne; Malcolm John, Jr.; Peter James;* the parents in the middle: *Malcolm John Bonner* and *Grace Elizabeth Bonner;* and *Margaret Jane.* And on the other side of the crease the name he had been waiting to read: *Coley Joe.*

"It's you! It's really you, Coley Joe!" Andy whispered, and he quickly turned the photo over to study the face that was so much like his own.

Coley Joe didn't look like a desperado of the Old West. He looked like a guy who was friendly and full of fun. The others in his family stared solemnly at the photographer, but the corners of Coley Joe's lips turned up as though he couldn't possibly hold back a smile.

"Whatever they said you did, I don't believe it," Andy told Coley Joe.

He dropped the photo onto the table and ran to the telephone, punching in J.J.'s number.

Mrs. Martinez answered and said, "J.J.'s doing his homework, Andy. Can he call you back?"

"I'll only be a second," Andy said. "I've got something I have to tell him right now."

"Oh, sure," Mrs. Martinez teased. "Like you just this minute found out you won the lottery."

Andy laughed, his excitement growing. "Better than that. Please, can I speak to J.J.?"

"Hang on," she answered. "I'll tell him."

In less than a minute J.J. was on the phone. "You won the lottery?" he yelled.

"No, but it's just as exciting," Andy answered. "I found a photograph of Coley Joe."

"That's your big news? You've got a one-track mind." J.J. sounded disgusted.

"It's big news to me," Andy said. "And you know what? Coley Joe looks kind of like me. Or I guess I should say that I look kind of like him. I know he couldn't have been a bad guy."

"You can't tell from the way he looks," J.J. insisted. "It's only on TV and in the movies that the bad guys look like bad guys."

Andy wasn't the least bit discouraged by what J.J. had said. "I'm going to prove that Coley Joe was a good guy," he declared.

"Miz Winnie said she wouldn't answer questions

33

about him, and Miss Minna won't either. So how are you going to prove anything about him?"

"The same way Miz Minna did her research," Andy answered. "I'm going to hunt up Coley Joe on my dad's computer."

"If Coley Joe's own family won't talk about him, who else will?"

"How did Miz Minna find out things about some of her relatives?"

"Just like she said. She contacted libraries that had genealogy material. She researched old records, but she worked at it for years. And some of it was pure luck."

"I feel lucky," Andy answered.

J.J. waited a few seconds before he said, "Andy, that stuff Miz Minna was talking about—the clothes and carriages and all that—we can share it. You can use it for your report, too."

"Thanks," Andy said. "And anything like that I get from Miss Winnie, I'll share with you. I'm going over there now to ask her more questions."

"About Coley Joe?"

"No," Andy said, but he knew if he asked some of the questions the right way, Miss Winnie might give him some information about Coley Joe without realizing it.

Andy took the photograph upstairs, propping it among the model planes that covered the top of his dresser. He smiled back at the photo of Coley Joe, who wore the hammered nail on a leather thong. Andy fingered the matching nail he wore, wondering which Bonner it had belonged to. He tucked the nail down inside his T-shirt. "Wish me luck, Coley Joe," he said.

Miss Winnie smiled as Andy opened his notebook across his lap and said, "Were you born here in Hermosa, Miss Winnie?"

"Yes, indeed," she said. "And my father before me."

"What year were you born?"

Miss Winnie stared up at the ceiling. "Oh, now, I don't think that's important, do you?"

"Sure I do," Andy said. "Mr. Hammergren told us to get dates whenever we could. If I write about what life was like when you were young, it wouldn't mean anything if I didn't have a date."

Miss Winnie sniffed. "This Mr. Hammerhead—he's a real busybody, isn't he?"

"It's Hammergren, and he's teaching us to collect facts."

"How many people are going to read this report?"

"Just Mr. Hammergren, far as I know."

Miss Winnie's forehead and lips puckered, but she said, "Well, all right, as long as this information doesn't get passed on to certain parties, like Minna Gasper, who might be under the impression I'm a year younger than I really am." She paused and took a deep breath. "I was born May 6, 1910."

"Wow!" Andy exclaimed.

"It's hardly the Dark Ages!" she snapped.

Andy tried to smile. "I just meant 'wow,' like in, 'Wow, May's a really terrific month to get born in.' That's all."

She fluttered a hand at him. "Hmmph! Who do you think you're kidding? Get on with the questions, Andy boy."

"Yes, ma'am," he said. "Your father was born in Hermosa, but how about your grandfather, Malcolm John junior?"

"Oh, my, no!" Miss Winnie exclaimed. "The Bonners came out of Virginia to settle in Corpus Christi when my grandfather was in his teens. Corpus Christi was a trading port, and Malcolm John senior hoped to find opportunity there."

"Did he?"

"Yes, he was successful, but you know the rest. Grace Elizabeth's health declined in the high humidity, and they had to move."

"What year was that?"

"It was 1879."

Andy thought a moment: *That was three years after the photograph had been taken. In 1879, Coley Joe would have been twenty-three years old.*

36

"The whole family came?"

Miss Winnie's lips tightened, and she looked at him warily, but Andy smiled and held his pencil up, ready to write.

"Yes. Malcolm John and his wife, Grace Elizabeth, with their two boys and two girls."

That leaves out Coley Joe, Andy thought. He made a note, then asked, "What kind of a house did they live in?"

"You understand that Hermosa was not much of a town at that time, don't you?" Miss Winnie asked.

When Andy nodded, she continued. "At first the Bonners marked the boundaries of their land. Then they stretched tarpaulins out, like tents, and built an enclosed shed to protect their two horses."

"They built a shed to house their horses before they built a house for themselves?"

"Of course. Besides the fact that the welfare of the horses was their responsibility, the horses were also their only means of transportation. There would have been no way to travel back and forth from their jobs in town without the horses."

Andy asked questions about the first house built on the Bonner property and about the house Miss Winnie had been born in. He made notes about the country store, with its pickles in one barrel, its crackers in another, and its peppermint sticks for the children who could afford them. He wrote about oil lamps and dust storms and mosquitoes, high-buttoned shoes and poke bonnets and petticoats. He made a face as he scratched out the word *petticoats*. There was no way he was going to write about underwear.

Although he got lots of information from Miss Winnie, he continued to wonder about Coley Joe, who had disappeared from the Bonner family sometime during the three years between the date the photograph was taken in 1876 and the family's move to Hermosa in 1879.

He just couldn't push away the idea that it was during this same period the Bonners' money had been stolen.

Just as Miss Winnie had finished describing the church socials that were popular when she was young, Andy could no longer control his curiosity. "Did the Bonners know who stole their money?"

Startled, Miss Winnie clutched the arms of her chair. She demanded, "Whatever are you talking about?"

"You told me yesterday that Malcolm Bonner's family's money had been stolen. Did this have anything to do with crossing Coley Joe's name out of the family's Bible?"

"Andrew Thomas, I made it very plain to you that I have no intention of answering a single question about Coley Joe Bonner. Coley Joe and the theft . . . This is private information that is not to be bandied about. Our interview is over."

Andy suddenly understood Miss Winnie's negative attitude. *So they thought Coley Joe stole his family's money!*

Andy pictured Coley Joe's easy smile among his family; then he thought about how he—Andy—even looked like Coley Joe. "Did you ever think that he *didn't* do it?" Andy asked Miss Winnie.

"Enough!" An angry flush stained Miss Winnie's cheeks and nose.

Andy realized he'd gone too far. "I'm sorry for upsetting you, Miss Winnie," he said. "Thanks for the interview." He hurried out of the house and, in a few minutes, entered his own.

The phone rang. As Andy reached for it, his mother called to him from the living room, "Someone's been phoning and hanging up. Ask what number they're trying to reach."

"Hello?" Andy said into the phone.

An odd voice whispered, "Write your report the way you were told. Forget your snooping. You can take this as a warning."

"Hey!" Andy shouted into the phone. "Who is this?"

But the caller had hung up.

Andy replaced the receiver with trembling fingers and leaned against the kitchen cabinet. That weird, whispery voice had scared him.

CHAPTER FIVE

"Who was it?" Andy's mother called.

"I dunno," Andy answered. He thought about the whisper, trying hard to identify the voice, but he shook his head in frustration. The voice could have belonged to a man or a woman . . . or a kid.

He telephoned J.J., trying to see if his pal could help figure out why such a thing would happen.

"Maybe it was somebody trying to be funny," J.J. suggested.

"It wasn't meant to be funny. Help me think. Only you and me, Miz Minna and Miss Winnie know that I'm trying to find out about Coley Joe."

"And Mr. Hammergren and everybody in our history class!" J.J. said. "You blabbed about your mystery man to everybody."

Embarrassed, Andy said, "I didn't mean to. I didn't say his name." He thought a moment. "I don't think it matters. None of them would care anything about Coley Joe."

"You said your relative was a mystery man," J.J. said. "Somebody in our class is going along with the gag."

"You're probably right." Andy began to relax. "At least I found out why the Bonners were so mad at Coley Joe. They thought he stole their money."

"You found that out. Now forget about him."

"Wait a minute, J.J. You knew all along, didn't you?"

"Sure. Miz Minna's talked about it, but it's no big deal."

"You didn't tell me. That's a big deal to me."

"Andy, we're best friends. Why should I tell you about one of your relatives, especially if it's a story that might make you feel bad. I hoped you wouldn't find out."

"If I'm going to hunt down Coley Joe, I need all the help I can get."

"What are you going to do next?"

"I've got kind of an idea, but I don't know yet if it will work," Andy said. "I'll tell you if it does."

"Okay. Want to go with me to the cemetery?" J.J. asked.

"What!"

"I liked Mr. Hammergren's idea about looking at the tombstones to see what's written on them. There are lots of Gaspers buried there and Bonner and Thomas relatives, too." As Andy hesitated, J.J. said, "Come on. It will get your mind off Coley Joe."

Visiting the cemetery was not Andy's idea of how to spend an afternoon. But J.J. was his best friend. "When do you want to go?" Andy asked.

"How about tomorrow, right after school? Ride your bike to school, and we can go from there."

"Okay," Andy said. "See you."

As Andy hung up the phone, his mother came into the kitchen. He mentioned their plan to her. "J.J. and I are going to ride our bikes to the cemetery tomorrow after school." Her eyebrows rose, so he quickly explained, "It's part of our history project, getting information from the old tombstones."

"Maybe I should go with you," she said. "That old part of the cemetery is off by itself, and I don't think it's very well patrolled."

"Mom!" Andy said. "I'm in the seventh grade, and I do not need my mother to follow me around, like I was a baby."

"Last year they picked up some out-of-towners selling drugs back behind the tombstones."

"The police chased them off. Okay? They haven't come back. Okay?"

When she didn't answer immediately, Andy said, "Mom, what's J.J. gonna think if you come with me?"

"We'll talk it over with your father after dinner," she said.

After dinner was a good time, Andy agreed. His dad came home hungry from his job as a pharmacist at the drugstore, and he was much more likely to agree to something—anything—when his stomach was full.

During dinner Andy fidgeted and squirmed, unable to enjoy the pot roast with potatoes and carrots that his mom had made. Impatiently waiting until he could bring up the trip to the cemetery, Andy studied his father's face. It was a nice face, with a squared jaw and crinkly smile lines at the outside corners of his eyes . . . like Grandpa Zeke's. And if Dad had a long, dark mustache, like the first Malcolm John Bonner's . . .

Mr. Thomas wiped his mouth with his napkin and said, "Okay, Andy, you can stop squinting at me now and tell me the problem. Have I got gravy on my chin? A fly on my nose?"

"Nothing like that, Dad," Andy said. "I was just figuring out that you could look a lot like Malcolm John Bonner if you had a long, droopy mustache with the ends turned up."

"Hmmm. Maybe I'll grow one," Mr. Thomas said.

"No, you won't," Mrs. Thomas said.

"Dad," Andy quickly told him, "I want to go to the cemetery with J.J. It's for homework." He briefly explained about the history assignment.

Mr. Thomas chuckled. "When I was a kid, a bunch of us went to the cemetery and sat among those old tombstones. We were determined to spend the night, just to prove how brave we were."

"Cool," Andy said. "I didn't know you spent the night in a cemetery."

"Actually, I didn't. Somebody got the bright idea of telling a really gruesome ghost story, and we all got so scared we went home. It wasn't even ten o'clock."

Andy laughed. "J.J. and I don't want to go at night. We just want to go after school."

His mom broke in. "Bill, that cemetery is awfully isolated—especially the old part. And remember, last year the police arrested some people selling drugs back in there where they thought no one would see them."

"Mom thinks we wouldn't be safe. She wants to go with us." Andy looked pleadingly at his father.

Bill Thomas smiled at his wife. "Donna, I don't think there's any problem with the boys' going. It will be broad daylight, and that incident you mentioned is the only time they've had any trouble in the cemetery."

"Well . . ." She sighed and said, "Maybe I am being too protective. I suppose I shouldn't worry."

Andy grinned. "That means we can go! Thanks!"

As he jumped up to clear his plate from the table, his mother asked, "Andy, have you had time to go through all those papers in Miss Winnie's box?"

44

"Not yet," he said. "There's an awful lot of stuff in there, and it's all mixed up."

"I know," she told him, "which is why I thought when you sort through it, you could also catalog it for her."

"What?"

"You know, fasten all the letters together in a bundle, put the receipts of sale and copies of bills in folders, maybe another folder for the children's drawings and letters."

"Mom! That would take forever!"

"No, it wouldn't. And it would be a good way to repay Miss Winnie for her kindness in helping you."

"I second the motion," Mr. Thomas said.

"Okay," Andy answered. He scraped off his plate and put it into the dishwasher.

"By the way," his mother said. "While you're at the cemetery, look for Malcolm John Bonner's headstone. It's not very large, but it's an unusual dark red. It's been years since I've seen it, but I remember that it struck me at the time that there's something odd carved on it."

"Odd? Like what?" Andy stared at his mother.

"I don't remember," she said. "When you find out, remind me."

As she began talking to his father about a sale on men's shirts at Gaspers' Department Store, Andy picked up his backpack to go to his room.

Mr. Thomas looked up. "Going to do your homework? Good."

"Dad," Andy said, "you've got AOL and World Wide Web and all that on your computer. Does it have a genealogy board someplace in it, too?"

"Oh yes. I know of many genealogy sites on the Internet."

"Can you show me how to use it?"

"I will help you. But you'll have to do the research on your own," Mr. Thomas said. "You know about Yahoo, right? It's a great place to start your research on the World Wide Web. Check my *favorite places* icon, but I think the address is http://www.yahoo.com/. Once the site appears, type *genealogy* and you're on your way." He thought for a moment. "What do you hope to find?"

"Miz Minna used her genealogy message board to find a couple of cousins she'd never heard of before, who gave her information about some major in the Civil War."

"I don't think it's going to be as easy as it sounds to turn up relatives."

Andy shrugged. "Just let me give it a shot. Okay, Dad?"

"Of course. Good luck," his father answered. "But remember, don't give anyone your name or address. If you have to give a name, stick to a screen name."

Once the computer service had connected, Andy

46

typed in his father's ID and current password, which were printed on a file card tucked under the keyboard.

He jumped to Yahoo and typed in the keyword, *Genealogy*. Up came a list of possible choices. Andy groaned. Miz Minna hadn't told him about all this. His father was right. Research was not easy. After more than an hour, Andy went into AOL and found "United States 1850 to Present." He clicked on it, pressed *enter,* and discovered a series of messages from people around the country.

Someone asked if Oliver Wendell Holmes had ever run for president of the United States. A teacher asked for recommended books about the Cold War and domestic politics since World War II. And someone wrote that in Massachusetts he'd found a memorial stone to Gerrit H. Niver, who was killed in the Custer Massacre at the Battle of the Little Bighorn, but Niver wasn't listed with Custer's soldiers. Did anyone have the answer?

Andy was surprised to read a message that answered the Niver question: Gerrit H. Niver had enlisted under the name of Gerritt von Allen, for some unknown reason, and was indeed killed with Custer in the battle.

"Cool," Andy murmured. At the end of the list of messages he clicked on the icon to create a message. As the blank screen came up, Andy wrote, "I'm using my father's computer for a history report I have to do about people in my family. There's a mystery person, someone no one will tell me about. His name is Cole Joseph Bonner, although he was known by the name of Coley Joe. He was born in 1856. His parents were Malcolm John and Grace Elizabeth Bonner, and they moved from Corpus Christi, Texas, to Hermosa, Texas, in 1879. Coley Joe's suspected of stealing his family's money. I don't think he did it. If you have any information, please write to me under my screen name, Hunter, at my dad's e-mail address, listed above. I need to find out more about Coley Joe. I really do."

He closed the history message board and clicked on the States, choosing the Texas board as the states' names came up.

He read through a number of messages from people trying to locate ancestors, then typed in the same message he had entered in the history board.

Next, Andy picked the alphabetical listing that would cover Bonner and went into the message board.

"Looking for John Billings," the first one read. "Born about 1861, married to Lucille James in Cincinnati, Ohio. Their daughter was Ellen Billings, married to Richard Burke. They were my grandparents, but I have no further information about them, and I can't find any information. Please contact me by e-mail if you know anything about them."

Andy clicked to the next message and read, "I'm looking for anything on my grandma's sister, Myrtle Bridges. Born 1907, grew up in an orphanage in Virginia. Last news was over fifty years ago when she married an Arthur Davis. My grandma's name is Emily. Their parents' names were Dorothy and Edwin Bridges. Please answer by e-mail."

The hands of the clock on the desk were moving fast. Andy took a deep breath and added his message a third time. As he clicked on *send,* he worried that he'd said too much and been too insistent.

For the next five minutes Andy waited for the mail symbol to appear, which would let him know his message had been answered, but nothing happened.

Andy disconnected the service, then turned off the computer. He slumped back in the chair. Had he really believed that some kind of magic would pull someone out of the sky to answer his questions about Coley Joe? What he had done made just as much sense as his pleading to be able to go to the cemetery—the last thing on earth he really wanted to do.

Andy went into the kitchen. *I've got to outline an essay for English class and do a page of problems in math,* he told himself. *There's no way I'll have time to start organizing the stuff in that box.* But he found himself walking to the box and plunging his hands in, wiggling his fingers through the papers to the bottom of the box. The tips of his fingers rubbed against soft leather—a small, rectangular packet—which he pulled out of the box.

The worn leather, so old it had blackened, was smooth in Andy's hands. He placed the packet on the counter and opened it. It was divided into thirds. Tucked into the left-hand side was a cracked and badly faded photograph of a woman, her dark hair pulled tightly back and wound into a coil that rested against her shoulders. She was not smiling. In fact, her eyes looked sad, but there was a wistful softness to her face. She sat upright, facing the camera and clutching a small book in her hands. Andy recognized her. She was older than in the family photograph, but she was definitely Grace Elizabeth Bonner, Coley Joe's mother.

He looked at the book she held, then pulled from the box the small poetry book his mother had mentioned. It was too hard to tell, without a magnifying glass, if this was the same book. But Andy was pretty sure the Bonner family hadn't been able to buy many books.

Andy had never been very much interested in poetry. Some of it was too hard to figure out. Besides, he thought, if a person had something to say, why not just say it and be done with it? Why hunt around for a word to rhyme it with?

He put the poetry book back into the box and examined the packet. Inside one fold were official-looking certificates. When Andy had them smoothed out to read, he could see that they were certificates of death. Grace Elizabeth's, Victoria Grace's, and Rose Marie's.

With a sudden pang, as though these were friends he

had known, Andy solemnly refolded the papers, put them where they had been, and closed the packet. As he carefully placed it back inside the box, his fingers touched the poetry book, and he found himself picking it up again.

I don't read poetry, Andy reminded himself, but he took the book with him as he headed upstairs to do his homework, placing it on the nightstand next to his bed.

By bedtime, his head filled with math problems, Andy had forgotten about the book. He wadded his pillow into just the right shape, wiggled and curled into a comfortable ball, and immediately fell asleep.

Sometime during the night Andy dreamed. This dream wasn't the hodgepodge that usually ran through his head. As clearly as though it were day, Andy watched a woman pull a chair next to his bed and sit in it. Her dark hair was streaked with gray and fastened tightly into a knot at the back of her neck. She leaned forward, her eyes never leaving Andy's face. Her gaze was deep, with such an intense pleading that Andy squirmed.

He recognized the woman from her photograph. She was Grace Elizabeth Bonner.

With both hands Grace Elizabeth clutched a small book to her chest, as if she were afraid of losing it. But slowly her fingers relaxed, and she held out the book toward Andy.

"No," Andy mumbled, afraid of her closeness and of the way her eyes kept searching his. "No. No. No!"

But Grace Elizabeth persisted, thrusting the book toward him.

"No!" Andy yelled.

"Andy? Are you all right? Are you having a nightmare?"

Andy struggled to sit up as his mother came into the room and sat on the edge of his bed. She reached out a hand to feel his forehead, but Andy ducked. "I haven't got a fever, Mom. I'm not sick. I just had a nightmare. I'm okay."

His mother smiled. "Maybe the nightmare came from something you read."

Andy followed his mother's gaze and saw that Grace Elizabeth's poetry book no longer rested on the nightstand. He was clinging to it with both hands.

CHAPTER SIX

When he awoke to sunlight the next morning, Andy tried to figure out if his dream had a special meaning. The dream didn't seem to make any sense. He tucked the book into the drawer of his nightstand, making sure it was securely closed.

Andy hung around after history period, until the classroom had cleared. He joined Mr. Hammergren, who had begun erasing what had been written on the board.

"How's it going, Andy?" Mr. Hammergren asked.

"Okay, I guess," Andy said. "J.J. and I are going to ride out to the cemetery after school to look at family tombstones."

Mr. Hammergren turned and smiled. "I hope you find something interesting. Do you know that some people even visit graveyards on vacations, searching for some of the old stones?"

"On vacation?"

"Sure. I remember a couple of tombstones I saw. In an old Western cemetery, under one man's name was 'Caught stealing the Marshal's horse. Sam never did have good sense.'

"And I like this one, from a cemetery in Medway, Massachusetts, 'Beneath this stone a lump of clay, lies Uncle Peter Daniels, who too early in the month of May, took off his winter flannels.' "

Andy smiled. *Maybe that's what Mom meant when she said something odd was carved into Malcolm John Bonner's tombstone.* He hoped it was something funny. *Odd* made it sound scary. *Funny* he could live with.

"Could I tell you something confidential?" Andy asked.

"Sure." Mr. Hammergren sat on the edge of his desk and gave his full attention to Andy. "I'm listening."

"It's confidential," Andy said, "because of my great-aunt. Because she'd get mad if people knew—I mean like people who couldn't keep things secret." Andy took a deep breath and told Mr. Hammergren all about Coley Joe.

"I don't know how, but I'm going to find out about Coley Joe and what really happened," Andy said.

Mr. Hammergren thought a moment. "Okay, let's look at the facts you've come up with: This relative

54

named Coley Joe disappeared, he was cut out of the family, and his father's money was stolen. It wouldn't take the police long to figure this one out."

"But I believe he didn't do it, and I have to prove it. The only trouble is that I don't know what to do next."

"Two heads are sometimes better than one," Mr. Hammergren said. "This head is asking what you'd do if someone disappeared."

"I'd go looking for him."

"Where was he going when he disappeared? See if you can retrace his route."

Andy thought so hard he frowned. "The family was planning to move to Hermosa. The father had bought land here, and he was going to buy cattle and build a ranch house. Only he couldn't, with the money gone."

"It's possible that Coley Joe was sent ahead of his family to buy livestock and the materials for building a house so that when the rest of his family arrived they'd have a roof over their heads."

Andy gasped. "You mean he really might have come to Hermosa?"

"He might."

Andy shook his head. "But then he would have done what his family wanted him to do. I don't think he ever got to Hermosa."

"In 1879 or thereabouts, you said. Hmmmm. The logical thing for Coley Joe to do would have been to head for El Paso, which was the major city nearest to

55

Hermosa. He could have planned to buy his stock there and hire help to move the cattle to the family's land.

"On the other hand," Mr. Hammergren added, "he might have kept going west after he reached El Paso, striking out on his own. To many the West Coast was a promised land."

"I don't think Coley Joe took the money," Andy said. "If there's any possible way to find out, I will."

"Why?"

Andy was startled. "Why? Well, I like Coley Joe. I want to clear his name. It must have been awful for his family to cross him out of the family's Bible and to pretend all these years that he didn't exist. That's why."

Mr. Hammergren smiled. "I like what you're doing, Andy. Keep me informed. And if you want to talk about your progress or ask questions, don't hesitate to ask me."

"Thanks," Andy said.

"One more thing," Mr. Hammergren told him. "If you want any lunch at all, you'd better hurry. You've only got fifteen minutes left."

Heavy clouds, dark as mud, clotted the sky by the time Andy and J.J. arrived at the cemetery.

"It's going to rain," J.J. said.

"Not for a while," Andy said. He rested his bike against the wrought-iron fence, laid his helmet in the basket, and peeled his sweaty shirt from his back. "At least when it's cloudy it's not so hot."

"What's that around your neck?" J.J. asked.

Andy touched the pounded nail. In spite of the heat, it was cold next to his skin. "A horseshoe nail," he said, and explained to J.J. what it meant.

"Cool," J.J. said. He led the way into the cemetery and took the path that wound through the neatly clipped, grassy area, with its flat grave markers, back over a small rise to the older part of the cemetery.

Wide, squatty tombstones crowded next to tall, imposing ones, most of them decorated with sculpted vines and crosses carved from speckled black-and-gray granite or pitted yellow sandstone. Here and there a weathered marble angel bowed his head and spread his wings.

In the center rose an ornate obelisk with a pointed top. It made Andy think of a giant's finger reaching from the earth to forever point upward.

J.J. stopped so suddenly that Andy plowed into him. "That's where James Jonathan the first is buried," J.J. said. "It looks like those obelisks we saw in the book about Egypt."

Andy had to lean back to see all the way to the top. "Was the first J.J. Egyptian?"

"Nope," J.J. said, and grinned. "I think he just wanted his tombstone to be more important than everyone else's."

To his right Andy heard a *plink,* like rock hitting rock, and he jumped.

"What are you scared of?" J.J. asked. "Nobody's here but us."

A jackrabbit shot out from behind two stones, its long back legs thrumming against the ground as it dashed to safety. Andy watched the jackrabbit's progress until it leaped from the rise down to the flat prairie that stretched to the horizon. The low scrub, mottled in gray green and purple, was dotted in the distance with grazing cattle—much like the Bonners' ranch.

"Nobody but us and the jackrabbits." Andy realized his laugh was shaky.

J.J. pulled a notebook and pencil stub from the pocket of his jeans. "I'm going to read what's written on all the Gasper family stones," he said. "Do you know where your Bonner family stones are?"

"I can find them," Andy said. "Mom gave me directions." As he turned right and moved into the thickly clustered tombstones he heard the same soft *plink* again. Was someone back in there? Someone moving among the graves?

The clouds grew darker, completely cutting off the straggly remnants of sun. A cold, crawling sensation slid up Andy's backbone, and he shouted back to J.J., "Don't take too long! Okay? We want to get home before it starts to rain."

Malcolm John Bonner's tombstone was nothing

more than a plain, rectangular block, but the dark red-and-black speckled granite stood out like a splotch of dried blood against the gray-flecked granite and yellow sandstone markers that surrounded it.

Silently, Andy approached the stone. Deeply carved were Malcolm John's name and dates of birth and death. At first, Andy saw nothing else. Then, suddenly, down in the right-hand corner of the stone, where long fingers of grass reached up to almost hide it, he made out a small carving of a snake's head. Its mouth was open, as though it were attacking, with its two sharp fangs thrust outward.

"Hey, J.J.!" Andy shouted. "C'mere! Quick!"

His shout seemed to vibrate in the quiet air, whamming and bouncing off the tombstones. A soft thud came from behind him, and he whirled, but no one was there.

J.J. appeared so suddenly that Andy jumped. "What's the matter?" J.J. asked.

"Look at this," Andy said, and pointed at the snake's head.

J.J. bent over to examine the carving and whistled. "Wow! Did Malcolm John Bonner die of snakebite? Is that why this snake head is carved here?"

"No one said anything about snakebite."

"Ask Miss Winnie."

A low roll of thunder rumbled from the near distance as the sky darkened.

J.J. held out his notepad to Andy. "I couldn't find anything interesting on the grave markers, just 'loving husband and father' and 'devoted wife and mother.'" He grinned. "If one of them got shot during a poker game, the Gaspers didn't put it on the tombstone."

Lightning flashed across the sky, and the next smack of thunder shook the ground.

"We need to get out of here," Andy said. "It's getting close."

But before Andy and J.J. could move, something round and dark leaped at them from behind the tombstones. Grunting, yelling words that Andy couldn't understand, a short, powerful figure grabbed his wrist and J.J.'s and ran, dodging the tombstones as he pulled the boys across the low hill and down to the covered porch of a small building.

As they slammed up against the wall, a bolt of blinding lightning smashed into the ground at the rise of the old cemetery.

"There! You see! You see! Right where you were standing!" the strange figure shouted. "You boys got grass growin' where your brains ought to be?"

Andy stared at a man who was not much taller than he was. His shoulders were broad, his arms muscular and overlong, and his body was round as a ball. The eyes that peered from within his wrinkled, weathered walnut shell of a face were a startling blue.

Thunder pounded against Andy's ears, and lightning

splattered white fingers into the dark sky. Crossly, the man said, "Stop gawkin' like a pair of stupid, cud-chewin' cows and come on inside till the storm's passed."

Hesitantly, Andy entered as the man held the door wide open. J.J. followed.

The room was small and the furniture plain, but two of the walls were lined with bookshelves to the low ceiling, and all the shelves were crammed with books. A half-filled, sour-smelling cup of coffee rested on a wooden table.

"Sit down," the man said, pointing to the sofa, "and tell me what y'all are doin' in my cemetery."

"*Your* cemetery?" Andy blurted out.

"Yes, *my* cemetery," the man said. "I'm Elton, and I'm the caretaker here."

Together, in a scramble of words, Andy and J.J. tried to explain to Elton about their history project.

Finally Elton shook his head. "This ain't Boot Hill. None of them funny sayings are written on these stones."

"But there is something weird on Malcolm John Bonner's stone," Andy said. "Down at the bottom is carved a small snake head."

Elton nodded. "Know what it means?"

"No," Andy said.

"There's other words for snakes, you know."

"Like what?"

"Got a dictionary? Look it up. Then ask the right person."

Andy was bewildered. "What right person?"

"You ever hear tell of William Shakespeare?"

"Sure." Andy did a double take. "But I can't ask him anything. He's dead."

"That won't stop him none from answering your questions. Or Malcolm John Bonner, neither, for that matter."

Andy gulped. "You can't talk to the dead."

Elton leaned forward and grinned, his teeth gaping like little brown nutmeats, as he chuckled soft and low. "I can," he said. "That's how I know why Malcolm John Bonner ordered that snake head to be carved on his stone."

"C'mon. You're kidding, aren't you?" Andy heard his voice tremble.

Elton swept an arm toward the cemetery that lay outside his door. "Kidding? Not on your life. There's nobody around here but me and the dead. Who else have I got to talk to?"

CHAPTER
SEVEN

At the dinner table that evening Andy said, "After school me and J.J. rode our bikes out to the cemetery, but it started to rain hard and thunder and lightning. We sat in the caretaker's house until the storm was over."

"Good thinking," his dad said.

"J.J. and I." Andy's mother corrected him.

"Elton said he talks to the dead. Do you believe he can do that?" Andy put down his fork, waiting for an answer.

"Far as I know, he could talk to anybody," Mr. Thomas said. "The big question is, do the dead talk back?"

"Bill!" Mrs. Thomas said. "What a thing to say!"

"Maybe they do." Andy laughed but shivered.

63

"Mom, the odd thing at Malcolm John Bonner's grave is the snake head with the big fangs carved near the bottom of the tombstone. You told me there was something strange on the stone, remember?"

"A snake," his mother murmured. She squinted as though she were trying to see the stone again. "That's right. I'd forgotten. It was a snake."

"Not a whole snake. Just a snake head," Andy said. More at ease now that his parents were involved in the story, he took a mouthful of mashed potatoes; then he continued. "Elton said there were other words for snake. He told me to use the dictionary. He said William Shakespeare is probably the best way to understand. I've only read *Romeo and Juliet,* and not even the whole play. Next year we read *A Midsummer Night's Dream.*"

"Shakespeare," his father said. "That's interesting. What are words for snake? *Reptile . . . serpent . . .*"

"Serpent!" Mrs. Thomas smiled. She looked pleased with herself as she said, "Perhaps Elton's referring to *King Lear.* 'How sharper than a serpent's tooth it is to have a thankless child.' I still remember that quote from freshman English in college."

"What would that have to do with Malcolm John Bonner?" Andy asked.

"I have no idea," Mr. Thomas said.

"Maybe we should ask Miss Winnie if she knows what the snake head means," his mother added.

"No!" Andy realized he'd answered too loudly. As his parents looked at him with surprise, he shrugged and hunkered down in his chair. "This is my school project," he said. "I should be the one to ask Miss Winnie."

"Of course." His mother nodded and smiled.

Andy wasn't about to bring up the subject with Miss Winnie. He realized his mother had already explained the identity of the thankless child. He was shocked to think of how hurt and unforgiving Malcolm John must have been to have ordered a carving of a snake head on his tombstone.

"Elton Gillie took over as caretaker from his grandfather. He probably inherited a passel of stories from the old man, too," Andy's father said.

"Do you think he knows why the snake head was carved into Malcolm John Bonner's tombstone?" Mrs. Thomas asked.

"Perhaps, or he's built some legend around it. Andy, you might find it interesting to talk to Elton again and discover what he knows."

"I'd just as soon he didn't." Andy's mother stood and picked up her plate and glass. "I didn't like the idea of Andy and J.J.'s going to the cemetery in the first place, and I don't like what Elton told them. Talking with the dead! That's creepy."

Andy tried to look upset, but secretly he agreed with his mother. He'd found the answer to his question because his mother remembered her freshman English! There'd be no reason to see Elton again.

Mr. Thomas pushed back his chair. "I need to do some work on my computer. You won't need it for a little while, will you, Andy?"

Andy shook his head. "It's my night to do the dishes, and after that I've got to interview Grandpa and Grandma."

As Andy put the last plate into the dishwasher, his dad came into the room. Holding out a sheet of paper, he asked, "I take it you're known in genealogy circles as Hunter?"

Andy's face grew warm. "You told me to use a screen name."

"Right," Mr. Thomas said. "Well, Hunter, you received an e-mail letter from MLB321 in Santa Fe, New Mexico. She's got some love letters for you."

"Da-aad! Cut it out!"

Mr. Thomas grinned. "I didn't say they were *to* you. I said they were *for* you. They're letters that someone named Coley Joe Bonner wrote to his fiancée—Felicity Strickland."

Andy gasped. He snatched the sheet of paper from his dad. His heart thumped with excitement, and it was hard to keep his fingers from trembling. "She says they're letters Coley Joe wrote from El Paso! On his way to Hermosa!" Andy looked up at his father. "MLB321 wants to know my name and address or fax number. She'll send me copies of the letters. Dad?"

"I think it's safe enough to give her the fax number, but stick to 'Hunter' for now." Mr. Thomas smiled. "Go ahead and answer her e-mail, before you squirm a hole right through the floor. I'll wait to use the computer until after you've finished."

His father had left MLB321's e-mail letter on the screen, so Andy clicked on *reply* and wrote to thank MLB321 for the offer. He gave his dad's fax number, then clicked on *send*. A picture of a mailbox popped up on the screen. The mailbox sprouted wings and seemed to fly off somewhere deep inside the computer.

Andy collapsed against the back of the chair he was sitting in, finally able to breathe normally.

Letters from Coley Joe! They were bound to tell him something or give a clue as to what had happened. How long would it take for copies of the letters to arrive by fax? Was MLB321 sitting at the computer now, waiting for his answer? Or was she the kind that booted up once a week in her spare time? "Come on, MLB321! Do something!" Andy mumbled.

The phone on the fax line rang. His father's fax machine beeped and went into action. Andy jumped to his feet, ran to the fax, and removed the sheets of paper as they came up. There were three letters, each addressed to "My Dearest Felicity" in a swirly, scratchy kind of handwriting that Andy found hard to read.

Mr. Thomas came into the room. "Are the letters going to be of any help with your project?" he asked.

"Project?" As he stared at the handwriting of an ancestor whose whereabouts had become a mystery, Andy realized he had forgotten he was searching because of his history assignment.

"Look, Dad!" Andy said, and waved the sheets of paper toward his father. "Real letters, written by Coley Joe."

"That's good?" Mr. Thomas asked.

"It's cool. Really cool. All I have to do is figure out the handwriting so I'll know what he wrote."

"Have you thanked MLB321?"

"Ooops. I'll do that right now."

Andy went back to MLB321's e-mail letter, clicked on *reply,* and wrote: "Letters received. Thank you very much. Hunter."

He sent the mail and turned the computer over to his father. It was a terrible temptation to go up to his room and pore over Coley Joe's letters, but he had to keep his interview appointment with his grandparents. For safekeeping, Andy tucked the letters on top of the poetry book inside the drawer of his nightstand. He took a quick call from J.J. and filled him in before he ran across the lawn to his grandparents' house.

Grandma Dorothy ushered him into the den, where Grandpa Zeke, dressed in sweatpants and an old Dallas

Cowboys T-shirt, was stretched out in a recliner. Grandma Dorothy picked up the remote control and turned off the television set.

"Hey!" Grandpa Zeke exclaimed. "That blond girl from Idaho was just about to give the answer."

"We promised Andy we'd tell him family stories," Grandma Dorothy said. She sat in her armchair and smiled at Andy.

"Well, then, let's get it over with," Grandpa Zeke said. "That hospital soap opera's coming on next, and I don't want to miss it."

Grandma Dorothy smiled at Andy. "Your grandpa's just kidding," she said. "Go ahead, Andy. Ask whatever you like."

Andy gulped. "I forgot my notebook."

"Looks like you forgot your pen, too," Grandpa Zeke told him.

Andy looked at his empty hands, surprised. "I'm kind of excited," he said. "I just got something special faxed to me."

"A course on how to improve your memory?" Grandpa Zeke asked.

"Now, Zeke, don't try to fluster the boy," Grandma Dorothy said. She got up and fished through the top desk drawer until she found a notepad and pencil. "Here," she said to Andy. "You can use these."

"Thanks, Grandma," Andy said. He looked toward

the screened porch and lowered his voice. "Is Miss Winnie back there?"

"Miss Winnie's gone to bed," Grandma Dorothy said. She settled back into her chair.

Andy leaned forward, lowering his voice. "I asked about Coley Joe Bonner on the Internet's genealogy bulletin boards. I didn't use Dad's name. I used the name Hunter. A little while ago I got copies of three letters. They were written by Coley Joe Bonner to his girlfriend, back in Corpus Christi."

Grandma Dorothy blinked, then frowned. "I heard Miss Winnie tell you not to question her about Coley Joe Bonner."

"I'm not questioning her, Grandma. I'm trying to clear Coley Joe's name. Do you know about Coley Joe and that his family thought he stole their money?"

"Yes, I know the family story. But the Bonners didn't just *think* Coley Joe stole their money. They had some kind of proof."

"Proof? What kind of proof?"

"I have no idea. I doubt if Miss Winnie even knows. If she does, she's never mentioned it to me."

Grandma glanced toward the hallway that led to Miss Winnie's bedroom. "I really wish you'd forget about Coley Joe," she said. "Every time you've mentioned him, it's upset Miss Winnie. She doesn't want anyone to know about him."

"Miz Minna knows. She said something about a

skeleton in the Bonners' closet. She said something about *proof,* too."

Grandma Dorothy sighed. "Over the years Miz Minna has held the story of the theft over Miss Winnie's head."

"Why?" Andy asked.

Grandpa Zeke broke in. "Why? Because Miz Minna's family from way back has been livin' in high cotton. The Bonners, on the other hand, came to Hermosa poor and hungry, then made something of themselves. Miz Minna considers the Bonners upstarts. I guess she wants to keep Miss Winnie in her place and—"

"No more about Coley Joe," Grandma Dorothy declared. "Ask the questions you need for your report, Andy. We're ready to answer them. Did I ever tell you that when I was a little girl we didn't throw away socks that had holes in them? We learned to darn the holes with tiny, woven stitches."

Andy heard about outhouses and when electricity first came to rural West Texas and having to memorize the multiplication tables through twelve. Grandpa Zeke's story about the first time he milked a cow and got his milking stool kicked over made Andy laugh. And his mouth watered as Grandma Dorothy described kneading and slicing homemade fudge, which her parents gave to all the near neighbors and friends at Christmas.

"Got enough information, Hunter?" Grandpa Zeke asked. He winked as he used the remote control to turn on the television set. "It's nine o'clock, and my program's on now."

Andy smiled as he got to his feet. "You gave me a lot of good background," he said. "Thanks."

"You're welcome," Grandma Dorothy said as she escorted Andy to the front door. "If you come up with any more questions, we'll be glad to answer them."

She placed a hand on Andy's shoulder and paused, glancing with a worried frown toward Miss Winnie's bedroom. "But please, Andy. Do me a big favor. Please forget all about Coley Joe."

Andy smushed and crackled his way across the leaf-strewn lawn, remembering too late his intention of raking the leaves for Grandpa Zeke. *Saturday,* he told himself. *Saturday would be a good day.*

Once up in his bedroom, Andy yanked the copies of Coley Joe's letters from the drawer and spread them on his desk. He pulled the magnifying glass out of a "young detective" kit his grandfather had given him on his eighth birthday. So far, all he'd done with the kit was use the glass, along with the sun, to set dried leaves on fire.

"Hey!" Andy laughed. "I'm being a detective right now!" He bent to scan the words through the glass. He could make out the narrowest, threadlike sweeps, and he saw where tiny ink blots widened some of the letters. Before long, as if he were learning a foreign language, Andy began to feel at home with the spidery writing and understand it.

The letters were dated the first, eighth, and fourteenth of December 1877.

The first letter began:

My Dearest Felicity,
    I think of you night and day and long to return to Corpus Christi to claim you as my bride.

Andy grimaced. He wished Coley Joe had written straight, plain letters, without turning so mushy over some girl.

Coley Joe went on to describe the rigors of his trip to the noisy, dusty town of El Paso across the miles of scrub-covered prairie.

In his second letter, along with the yucky love stuff, he wrote of widespread gambling in El Paso and numerous saloons—"too many to count."

His third letter told of making a friend, "a learned gentleman," who worked as chief clerk for a district judge. Coley Joe wrote:

My friend has offered his help and promises to ride with me to San Elizario, near El Paso, to meet with a gen-

*tleman who wishes to sell a herd of Longhorn cattle. A
chief clerk's job is highly respectable but, alas, pays only
a small salary, so he is hoping to collect a commission.*

Coley Joe went on into a boring comparison of the
hardiness and disease resistance of the Longhorn, versus
the more flavorful and tender meat of the Angus.

The third letter ended:

*I pray that time will pass quickly, my love, so that we
may once again be together.*

Andy put down the letters and thought hard about
what he'd read. He dismissed all the details and focused
on the fact that Coley Joe had arrived safely in El Paso
and had fully intended to purchase livestock for his family's future ranch in Hermosa.

He wasn't running away with the money, Andy told
himself. *He'd promised Felicity Strickland he'd come back to
marry her.* Probably a bad move, but Coley Joe had
seemed set on it. Andy was sure that Coley Joe wasn't
the kind to make promises, then break them.

Andy gathered up the pages to return them to the
drawer in his nightstand. He had his hand on the drawer
pull when he froze, gasping at the sight of the faded
blue poetry book. It lay not inside the drawer where he
was positive he had left it but on the nightstand next to
his pillow.

Exasperated because he couldn't remember handling

the book, Andy stuffed it inside the drawer, laid the copies of Coley Joe's letters on top of it, and shut the drawer tightly. He had to think about what he'd just found out. And he had to sleep. There was no room in his life for more bad dreams!

CHAPTER EIGHT

"So how are y'all coming with your family reports?" Mr. Hammergren asked the next morning in history class.

"Are we supposed to start them already?" Harvey asked.

"When did you say they're due? I forget," Nelson asked.

Tiffany Lamb waved a hand. "I'm making a family tree to go with my report. I've gone back four generations."

Harvey groaned. "Is that something we gotta do?"

"No, it's not something you have to do," Mr. Hammergren said, "but Tiffany's idea is a good one. If you're collecting stories about a lot of grandparents and great-grandparents, it's a way of keeping their names straight."

"Does a family tree actually look like a tree? What does it look like?" Lee Ann asked.

"Tiffany? Why don't you show us?" Mr. Hammergren asked.

Tiffany hurried to the board and wrote her name on the left side in the middle of the board. Then she drew lines leading to her parents' names, and lines from them to her grandparents' names and their parents'. There were extra lines leading to names she identified as uncles and aunts. "And these are the names of who they married and their children, and then their husbands and wives and their children." Pretty soon her handwriting covered the board.

"It doesn't look like a tree. It looks like a spaceship," Luke said.

Andy took notes. Maybe if he went all the way back to Malcolm John and Grace Elizabeth and wrote down all the begats—as Miss Winnie called them—there'd be a pattern that might fit together. It was worth a try.

"Anyone else want to share what they're doing?" Mr. Hammergren asked. "I'd like to hear what directions you're taking."

"I sent out a query over the Internet," Andy said, "and got an answer. A woman faxed me three letters one of my ancestors wrote to his girlfriend." He grinned. "Dad had told me not to use my real name, so I used the name Hunter."

Luke and Harvey hooted, but Mr. Hammergren said, "That was a neat idea, Andy. Are the letters going to help you with your project?"

"I think so," Andy said. "At least I know this guy made it to El Paso."

When the bell rang, Mr. Hammergren asked Andy to wait a few minutes.

"Why don't you stick around with me, J.J.?" Andy asked.

"We're going to be late for lunch," J.J. complained.

"Hey, what are friends for?"

"Friends don't make friends miss lunch," J.J. said as his stomach growled, but he walked with Andy to Mr. Hammergren's desk.

"Are these letters from the guy who disappeared?" Mr. Hammergren asked Andy.

"Yeah. Coley Joe."

"So you did trace him to El Paso. Good for you."

"Thanks," Andy said. His stomach growled, and he turned toward the door.

"One second," Mr. Hammergren said. "How far are you going with this search for Coley Joe?"

"As far as I can," Andy said. "I hope I can find out how and why he disappeared."

"You've already found out he got to this part of Texas," J.J. said. "Isn't that enough?"

Andy stared at J.J. "You want me to give up?"

J.J. shrugged. "You know what happened next. Nothing is going to change the facts."

"Unless I find other facts that prove the first facts are wrong."

Mr. Hammergren broke in. "Let's see how your search progresses. If you can bring it to a conclusion, then I'm going to suggest you write an essay about it. There's a statewide history essay contest I'd like you to enter. First prize is a nice-sized college scholarship."

"A scholarship?" J.J. repeated.

Andy was puzzled as a strange expression came into J.J.'s eyes. He looked as if he were sorting out every thought that strayed into his head.

Finally, J.J. said, "And an automatic A on our history project?"

Mr. Hammergren chuckled. "You sound like Andy's agent."

"I have to be. We're best friends."

"Okay. An A on the project."

J.J. shrugged. "Deal."

Mr. Hammergren smiled at Andy. "A little fame might go with it, too. The winners are always written up in their local newspapers and are often on the local television newscasts. Think you can handle that?"

Andy laughed. "My mom would like it, but I wouldn't. She'd make me get a haircut and wear a shirt and tie."

"We'll negotiate," J.J. said. He tugged Andy to the classroom door. "C'mon. We've already missed ten minutes of lunch."

Andy had just enough time to turn and give Mr. Hammergren a thumbs-up. A statewide contest? A scholarship? Wow! He had more reason than ever to find Coley Joe.

As usual, Andy and J.J. walked home together. The row of white columns on J.J.'s front porch gleamed in the afternoon sunlight, and a single browned oak leaf spiraled lazily down to an immaculate green lawn. The air had the spicy smell of freshly cut grass and newly planted marigolds.

"Did Miz Minna put together a family tree?" Andy asked J.J.

"I dunno. Probably." J.J. looked curious. "Why?"

"Because I wrote down some of what Tiffany said about her family tree, but I can't remember where some of the people go who aren't in a direct line. I thought Miz Minna could show me."

"We can ask," J.J. said. "C'mon in."

Miz Minna shut down her computer as Andy and J.J. appeared at her open doorway. She rose with difficulty from her desk chair and hobbled with tiny steps to her large armchair by the window. Sinking into its soft curves and fat pillows, she said, "Y'all sit down, and watch what you're doing. Careful, Andy. There's a pitcher of water by your elbow. Don't tump it over." She held out a hand toward J.J., who dutifully bent to kiss her forehead.

Andy glanced at the computer. "We didn't mean to interrupt you, Miz Minna," he said.

Miz Minna smiled. "You didn't interrupt. I was just browsing. There are so many interesting Web sites to browse. And the number keeps growing. There's a senior citizens' board, you know. Why, last week . . . Would you like to hear about the topic that came up last week?"

J.J. got right to the point. "Sure, Miz Minna, but not right now. Andy's got something to ask you."

"About family trees," Andy said.

"What about them?"

Andy was puzzled about the edge that had come into her voice. "I want to write down a family tree for my family, and I think I know how to put together most of it, but there are some parts I'm mixed up about. Like what to do with leftover people."

"Leftover people?"

Andy put down his backpack and pulled out the notes he'd made from Tiffany's chart. "Here," he said. "You start with yourself. Then you go to your parents, and their parents, and keep going as far back as you can. But most of those people have other children. So what about all the brothers and sisters along the way and the people they marry and their kids? What do you do with them?"

"You include them, of course," she said.

Andy grimaced. "What if they don't fit on the paper?"

Miz Minna's laugh was like a tiny bell. "Their names might fill sheets and sheets of paper."

"I don't want to fill sheets and sheets of paper," Andy said. "I don't care that much about cousins and cousins of cousins. I only care about the Bonners down through my father." *And Coley Joe, of course,* he added to himself.

Miz Minna seemed to relax. She reached out and patted Andy's hand. "Don't look so discouraged. If you're interested only in a direct line from Malcolm John Bonner to you, then that's all you need to write down."

She giggled. "How will Miss Winnie feel, being left out?"

"Oh," Andy said. "I'd better put her in, too." He smiled. "But that won't be hard. Miss Winnie didn't get married or have any children, so there won't be a lot of names to deal with. Maybe I can squeeze her in with the others on just one page."

He tucked his notes into his backpack and shrugged his arms into the straps. "Thanks, Miz Minna," he said, hoping she wouldn't decide to tell them about the senior citizens' bulletin board. "I've gotta go home now and study for a test."

"Wait a minute, Andy," she said, and her little paperlike fingers pressed hard against his arm. "You haven't told me what else you found in Miss Winnie's box beside the Bonner family Bible."

"A lot of papers and letters and stuff and a poetry book," Andy said. "I told Mom I'd sort through it for Miss Winnie, but I haven't had time to do it yet."

"Letters? What kind of letters?"

"Business letters, like to an attorney about buying more acreage. Stuff like that. Boring."

"If you find anything interesting, I'd like to learn about it. Y'hear?"

"Yes, ma'am," Andy said.

Andy didn't mention that everything he had found of interest so far had to do with Coley Joe. And he had no intention of talking about Coley Joe to Miz Minna, who had called Coley Joe a family skeleton in the Bonner closet.

The moment he arrived home, he booted up his dad's computer. As soon as he was on-line, he went into the genealogy bulletin board section and added another message: "This is Hunter again. I asked if anyone had any information about Coley Joe Bonner. Well, now I've got more facts to go on. Coley Joe arrived in El Paso at the beginning of December 1877. On December 14, he wrote that he was going with a friend to San Elizario, hoping to buy cattle. If anyone knows where Coley Joe might have gone after San Elizario, will you please e-mail me?"

He wrote the same message on the Texas bulletin board.

Would he get an answer? It was worth a try.

Andy exited Windows and leaned back in his dad's chair. He fingered the circular nail as he pictured Coley Joe's smiling face. *If you went to San Elizario,* he wondered, *did you buy cattle? And if you did, then what happened? Where did you take the cattle? Where did you go?*

Andy slowly got up from the chair and made his way to the kitchen. He poured a glass of milk, dumped a half dozen Oreos onto the table, and opened his math book. But he couldn't concentrate. The problems squiggled on the page like pairs of pesky little black lovebugs.

He locked the back door, jumped off the stoop, fastened his helmet, hopped on his bike, and headed for the cemetery. "I've got to talk to Elton and find out what he knows," he said aloud.

CHAPTER NINE

It took less than twenty minutes to pedal out to the cemetery. Andy was so intent on the questions he'd ask Elton that it didn't occur to him, until he approached the silent, lonely rows of graves, that he'd forgotten to leave a note for his mother. He hadn't even thought to ask J.J. to come with him.

Andy hesitated at the open gates, wondering if he should turn back and come another time—with J.J. for company.

"Back so soon?" a voice called. Elton stepped out from the doorway of his caretaker's house.

Andy removed his helmet, leaned his bike against the wrought-iron fence, and walked into the cemetery. "If you don't mind, there are a couple of things I'd like to ask you."

Elton grinned and motioned toward the door. "Come on inside. It's cooler."

Once inside Elton's living room, Andy sat where he had sat before on the lumpy sofa.

"I see you're wearin' the Bonner circle again." Elton nodded toward the thong and nail.

To Andy's surprise, it was hanging outside his T-shirt, in plain view.

"Want to know which Bonner it belonged to? Find the initials."

"What initials?" Andy asked. He pulled the thong over his head and studied the nail.

"Look on the nail head itself," Elton said. "You'll see some initials scratched in."

Andy squinted. Just as Elton had said, there were faint scratches. He could make out what looked like a tiny *M* and then a *J* and a *B*.

"Hand it over," Elton said. "I'll take a look."

He studied the nail and smiled. "Looks like you've got the old man's nail. Malcolm John Bonner himself."

Andy took a sharp breath and reached for the circle. The metal seemed warm against his fingers. "Maybe not," he murmured, saying the words while hoping he was wrong. "His son had the same name. It might have been his."

"Nope. His son would have had a *Jr.* scratched in."

This circle really had belonged to his great-great-

great-great-grandfather! Slowly, respectfully, Andy hung it again around his neck, this time tucking it carefully under his shirt.

"Next question?" Elton said.

"I didn't ask a question yet," Andy said.

"You was thinkin' it. Same thing. I suppose you want to know what the circle means."

"I think I know. Miss Winnie—my great-aunt—she told me that a circle means 'unbroken.' "

"Right. And these circles stood for an unbroken family circle. They all wore them—all the men in the Bonner family. Way I heard it, they was supposed to wear them forever, but old Malcolm, right there on his deathbed, tore his off. He told everybody he'd always hoped that Coley Joe would come back and return the money. But now it was too late. And then he said he wanted that serpent head carved on his tombstone so they'd all remember."

Andy shuddered. "How could he hate his son?"

"Wasn't hate. Just his own twisted kind of justice. Malcolm John felt betrayed."

"But lots of things could have happened to Coley Joe. Why was Malcolm so sure that his son had stolen the money?"

"I always heard there was proof."

"What kind of proof?"

"Now you gone past me with your questions. The

way the story goes, there was some kind of proof all right, but I never learned what it was. You got to find the answer to that one yourself."

"How?"

"I done told you once. Ask the dead. William Shakespeare's dead King Lear gave you one answer, didn't he?"

"Well, yes, in a way," Andy answered.

"So find out what the Bonners have got to tell you," Elton said.

"How?" Andy wailed.

Elton leaned back in his chair and scratched his stomach. "I made the first part pretty easy with my Shakespeare clue! I can't answer everythin' for you. Some things, like the big answers, you just gotta figure out for yourself."

That evening Andy raced through his homework and began to sort out the papers in Miss Winnie's box. There had been a few bad years, but mostly the Bonner ranch had thrived. Andy found countless bills of sale for livestock and for additional acreage.

You came out here owning nothing but land, he said to Malcolm John, *and you made a comfortable life for your family. You can be proud of that.*

But Andy pictured Coley Joe's smiling face and, for a moment, was swept into a dark well of sadness. *Why couldn't you have forgiven your son?* he thought. *What is this terrible proof that destroyed you?*

Andy didn't expect an answer, in spite of Elton's insistence that he should question the dead, so he wasn't disappointed when an answer didn't come. He sorted papers, fastening them together with rubber bands, until his mother came in to tell him it was time for bed.

Before Andy turned out the light, he sat on the side of his bed, his mouth still minty with the lingering taste of toothpaste. Slowly, he opened the drawer of his nightstand and sighed. Just as he had expected, the poetry book was in the drawer—but it was lying on top of the letters. Hadn't he put the letters on top? He'd meant to, but he couldn't remember.

Carefully, deliberately, Andy placed the letters on his nightstand and laid the poetry book on top of them. He pulled the leather thong from around his head and placed the circular nail on top of the book. "No more dreams. No more scary stuff," he said aloud. "I've got school tomorrow. I want to sleep."

But during the moments when he hung in an unreal haze between drowsiness and sleep, Andy heard Elton's voice saying once again, "Find out what the Bonners have got to tell you."

"Which Bonners?" Andy murmured.

No one answered.

Andy walked home by himself the next day, since J.J. had left school early for an appointment with his orthodontist.

Andy saw that their street-side mailbox was stuffed with the fall and early Christmas catalogs. He swept up the armful, carried it inside, and dumped it onto the kitchen table.

To his surprise, one of the envelopes had his own name and address printed on it, but there was no return address. As he stared at the thick block letters on the envelope, he felt that there was something ominous inside the envelope.

He didn't want to open it, but his curiosity won out. Andy reached into the nearest drawer, pulled out the letter opener, and slit the top of the envelope.

The block printing on the sheet of paper was the same as the address. The message was short:

HUNTER: THIS IS YOUR SECOND WARN-ING. BACK OFF OR YOU WON'T LIKE WHAT HAPPENS TO YOU.

Andy heard his mother's car in the driveway, stuffed the frightening threat back into the envelope, and shoved the envelope inside the waistband of his jeans, under his T-shirt. There was no way he was going to show the letter to his mom.

How could he explain this letter? He needed to talk to J.J. Andy glanced at the kitchen clock. J.J. should be home from the orthodontist by this time.

As Mrs. Thomas entered the kitchen, Andy dashed out. "Hi, Mom. Bye, Mom. Going to J.J.'s. Back before dinner!" he yelled.

Andy ran the entire way. J.J., who answered the doorbell, didn't even have a chance to say hello as Andy pushed him into the den.

"What's with you?" J.J. asked.

"I got this letter today. You have to read it." Andy pulled the letter from his shirt and shoved it into J.J.'s hands.

J.J. opened the letter while Andy collapsed on the sofa.

As he read the letter, J.J.'s eyes grew wide. "Who's this from?" he asked.

"I don't know. No return address."

J.J. plopped down beside Andy and stared at the letter again. "I think it's a joke—just like that warning you got over the telephone."

"Joke?" Andy sat upright, snatched the letter, and stuffed it back under his T-shirt. "Some joke!" He lowered his voice. "The letter writer called me Hunter. Only a few people know that name is mine."

"A few people, like everybody in class." J.J. grimaced. "You told everybody about using the name Hunter when you told them about getting the copies of Coley Joe's letters."

Andy stared at the letter. "I can't believe this is a joke."

"Okay, so who else did you tell?"

Andy frowned as he thought. "Mom and Dad, of course. And Grandpa and Grandma . . . and you."

"Maybe the letter came from your grandpa. He likes to tease."

"Threats aren't funny."

"Some of his jokes aren't, either, but he thinks they are."

A stray thought zapped Andy like the painful sting of a mosquito. He looked away from J.J. and climbed to his feet. "Thanks for reading the letter. I've gotta go."

"You just got here," J.J. said. "Why don't you stick around? We'll get something to eat."

"I'm supposed to rake leaves for my grandpa."

Andy headed toward the front door, J.J. following. "Hey, are you okay?" J.J. asked.

"Sure," Andy said. "I just forgot about the leaves, that's all."

He hurried out to the sidewalk and plodded for home, without a single backward glance.

"See you tomorrow," J.J. called.

"Sure. Tomorrow," Andy yelled, and waved a hand in J.J.'s direction.

He and J.J. had been best friends for years. Andy knew he'd told a number of people about using the name Hunter. That was no big deal. But the letter had spoken about a second warning, and—besides himself— nobody but J.J. knew about that first warning.

It hit Andy hard, but as far as he could figure out, only J.J., his best friend, could have written the letter.

CHAPTER TEN

A ndy raked not only Grandpa Zeke's lawn, but his own, amazing and delighting his parents and grandparents. As he came into the kitchen, he overheard his mother on the telephone saying to his grandmother, "You never know what to expect at this age. Sometimes they show such bursts of maturity."

Maturity? When all he wanted to do was rake leaves?

"There's nothing to eat in the refrig," Andy complained. He shut the door so hard two magnets and a note about a parent-teacher conference flopped to the floor. "How come there's never anything good to eat around here?" He bent over and wiped his dripping forehead with the edge of his sweat-stained shirt.

"Take a shower before dinner," his mother called.

"I was going to, Mom. You didn't have to tell me."

As Andy clomped out of the room, he heard his mother sigh and ask, "Does anyone understand boys at this age?"

At the moment Andy didn't care if anyone understood him or not. All he could think about was that something odd was going on with his best friend.

Had J.J. written the warning letter? And if he had, why? J.J. had talked about a joke. Was this his idea of a joke? Andy shook his head. A warning letter wasn't the kind of joke best friends played on each other.

Andy dawdled in the shower as long as he could, until his dad pounded on the door and said, "Your mother says come down to supper."

Within fifteen minutes Andy—hair still damp—slid into his chair at the kitchen table, where his parents were seated. Andy saw that his dad had almost finished eating, but his mother had been taking little bites, waiting for him to show up.

"Sorry I'm late," Andy said.

"It's okay," his dad said. "Thanks for raking the lawn."

"And Grandpa's lawn, too," his mother said cheerfully. She smiled at Andy's dad. "Bill," she said, "nobody even asked Andy to do the job. He chose to rake the leaves, all on his own. Isn't that wonderful?"

"We're proud of you, son," his father said.

They've been reading that psychology book about how to understand your teenager, Andy thought. His parents didn't know it, but he'd read it too, wanting to know what he was in for. *Praise the things that can be praised. Overlook the little problems.* Andy remembered that chapter. He grabbed his fork and lit into the meat loaf on his plate.

Mr. Thomas shoved a sheet of paper at Andy. "More e-mail for Hunter," he said.

Andy sat upright. "More of Coley Joe's letters?"

"Nope. You've got another correspondent. A DrPR. I guess, from the way he's chosen his ID, that he's a doctor."

"A doctor? What kind of a doctor?"

"Read and find out."

Andy read aloud, " 'Hunter: If you are a student of Texas history, you should know about the last battle of the Salt Wars that took place a few days after a public execution on December 17, 1877, in San Elizario. If you aren't familiar with the Salt Wars, go to your library. In the social sciences department, you'll find *The Handbook of Texas,* 976.4. In volume three read what C. L. Sonnichsen has written about the Salt Wars. Also, *The History of Texas,* by Bretze and Lehmberg, Noble and Noble, 1954, gives a brief account of the Salt Wars.' "

Andy put down the sheet of paper. "Dr. PR writes like a teacher. What's all that stuff about Salt Wars? What does that have to do with Coley Joe?"

"There's one way to find out," Mr. Thomas said. "Do what Dr. PR suggests. Go to the library."

Andy poked at his meat loaf as he tried to think. "Coley Joe wasn't a soldier, Dad. He wouldn't have gone off to fight in a war."

Mr. Thomas shrugged. "You asked a question, and somebody out there sent you an answer. Check it out. What have you got to lose?"

Glancing at the kitchen clock, Andy said, "I'll ride over to the library right after dinner."

"Bill," Mrs. Thomas said, "it's getting late. Why don't you drive him?"

"Aw, Mom," Andy said, "it won't be dark for a couple of hours. I'll be home long before then."

His mother and father gave each other a look. "I don't see anything wrong with that," his father said.

Mrs. Thomas sighed. "If you say so," she murmured, then turned to Andy. "Would you like dessert now or after your trip to the library?"

"After," Andy said.

As his mother began talking about what she'd wear to Saturday's opening night of Hermosa's Community Theatre, Andy wolfed down the rest of his dinner and pushed back his chair. "May I be excused . . . uh . . . please?" he asked.

"Of course," Mrs. Thomas said. "Watch the traffic. Be careful. . . ."

There was probably more, but Andy, who had grabbed his pen and notebook, leaped out the door and onto his bike. He fastened the chin strap on his helmet, raced down the driveway, and arrived at the James Jonathan Gasper Memorial Library within ten minutes.

It wasn't hard to find volume three of *The Handbook of Texas,* with the information about the Salt Wars. The library even had one old, slightly battered copy of *The History of Texas.* The information about the Salt Wars took up only a few paragraphs in each book. *No long, dry stuff to get through,* Andy thought, so he happily settled down to read and take notes.

Andy read carefully. Before settlers came to the El Paso area, there were shallow lakes, or "flats," at the foot of Guadalupe Peak, east of El Paso. These flats held great quantities of salt.

For years Native American tribes gathered the salt they needed, sharing without problems, until the white settlers arrived. At first, the settlers shared, too. But in 1869 two men—W. W. Mills and Albert J. Fountain—tried to acquire title to the salt deposits. They were opposed by a Louis Cardis, who controlled the local Mexican populace, and a Catholic priest—Father Antonio Borrajo of the nearby settlement of San Elizario.

In 1870 fighting broke out over the salt rights, and a Judge Gaylord Judd Clark was killed. Fountain moved to New Mexico, and for a few years there were no problems.

Then in 1874, Charles Howard, a former Confederate officer, became district judge. He filed on the Salt Lakes in the name of his father-in-law, Major George B. Zimpleman. This act outraged the citizens from Mexico, who felt they had a right to continue taking salt from the lakes.

In September 1877, when Howard arrested two men who had threatened to go for salt, a riot took place. Howard was held prisoner in San Elizario and was released only when he promised to give up his claim to the salt and leave the area.

He not only didn't keep his promise, but on October 10, Howard shot and killed Louis Cardis.

In the first days of December, sixteen wagons left for the Salt Lakes, but Howard brought suit against their owners and went to San Elizario to press charges.

At Howard's request he was protected from an angry mob by the Texas Rangers, but a battle began. Howard surrendered, believing he'd be freed, as did the Texas Rangers, who also surrendered. However, Howard and his two aides were shot by a firing squad, and San Elizario was looted by a mob.

Detachments of U.S. Army troops arrived in San Elizario, along with a posse of American citizens. Four men were killed, and a number were wounded.

The leaders and many members of the mob fled into Mexico. Indictments were made out against some of them, but no one was ever arrested or brought to trial.

The only action that was taken was by the U.S. Army in reestablishing Fort Bliss, which had been abandoned.

Andy leaned back in his chair, put down his pen, and rubbed his hand. *Okay. There was a war over salt. Howard and two aides were executed, but what did that have to do with Coley Joe?*

He read his notes over again, and as he reached the next to the last paragraph, he shuddered, a chill crawling up his spine. *Four men were killed, and a number were wounded.*

Coley Joe had written to Felicity that he was going to San Elizario with a friend. Coley Joe was new to the area, but the friend should have known about the bad situation in San Elizario. *Is it possible that Coley Joe was one of the men killed in that final battle?* Andy sat and wondered. *And if he was, what happened to his family's money?*

So many questions. He'd never find the answers. Andy slumped down in his chair, groaned, and clapped his hands over his eyes.

He jumped as someone touched his shoulder. Peering through his fingers, Andy saw the head librarian looking down at him. Mrs. Alonzo was a friendly middle-aged woman with soft eyes as dark as her hair. At this moment her eyes were filled with concern.

"Andy, are you all right?" she asked.

Andy nodded. "It's tough being a detective," he said.

Mrs. Alonzo sighed. "Right. It's tough being a librarian, too."

As she turned and walked away, Andy sat upright and closed the reference books. He had a lot of thinking to do and wasn't sure what was going to come next.

What would a real detective do? he wondered. He had seen enough private-eye movies to know that PIs wrote down the facts they came up with and added them all together. He could do that. Andy flipped to the next page in the notebook and began to write:

> *Coley Joe went to San Elizario just before the last battle in the Salt Wars.*
> *He went to buy cattle. Did he?*
> *He went with a friend.*

Andy stopped writing and read the last sentence over again. Who was Coley Joe's friend? How was he ever going to find that out? He began to write again:

> *Four men were killed at that last battle. Was Coley Joe one of them?*
> *Was his friend killed, too?*
> *If Coley Joe was killed, what happened to his family's money?*

There was nobody around who knew the answers to these questions, not even Elton, out at the cemetery. Andy read the paper over and groaned loudly. He folded his arms over his notebook, rested his head on his arms, and groaned again.

Once again Mrs. Alonzo's soft voice spoke over him. "Andy, are you sure you're all right?" she asked.

Andy sat up. "I've got a lot of questions without answers," he said.

Mrs. Alonzo smiled, pulled up a chair, and sat opposite him. "Well, I've got answers without any questions," she said. "Why don't we put our questions and answers together and see if any of them match?"

Andy thought a moment. Anything was worth a try. "Do you know about the Texas Salt Wars?" he asked.

"I can quickly find out. I see you've got one of the volumes in *The Handbook of Texas*. As I remember, it includes the Salt Wars."

Andy turned back a page in his notebook and slid it in the librarian's direction. "It does," he said. "Here are my notes."

She read the notes and looked up. "What's your first question?"

"The article said four men were killed. I need to know who they were."

"Okay," she answered.

"Okay?" Andy asked. "Okay? Just like that?"

"The answer isn't going to come flying through the window," she said. "It might take some digging to find it."

"I don't know where to start the digging."

She smiled. "I do. Look, both the U.S. Army and the Texas Rangers were involved in the Salt Wars. That means reports were filed."

Andy's mouth fell open. "All the way back in 1877?"

"Right."

"Would somebody still have them?"

"Most likely. That's the first thing we're going to find out."

"We?"

"Librarians don't just check books in and out," Mrs. Alonzo said. "We help our patrons."

A strange, excited, tingly feeling spread from Andy's back and up through his chest. He began to believe again that he really could find out what happened to Coley Joe.

"We're into the weekend," Mrs. Alonzo said, "so come by after school on Monday. I'm going to check with the Texas State Archives office in Austin and see what they can tell me."

"Cool," Andy said. "Thanks."

Mrs. Alonzo stood. "See you Monday," she said.

As Andy pushed through the outer doors of the library, he stopped short, startled that while he'd been in the library the sun had gone down. Streetlamps, office lights, and traffic signals gleamed and winked through the darkness.

A car's headlights picked up the red glow from the

reflectors on Andy's bike and helmet as Andy trotted down the steps to the bike rack. His mother wasn't going to like his being out after dark, so he'd better get home as quickly as possible. Andy hopped on his bike, fastened his helmet, and carefully pulled into traffic.

Within a few minutes Andy turned left off Gasper Street, taking a shortcut through residential streets. He picked up speed as his mind raced through what he'd learned and hoped to learn. Coley Joe, with a great deal of money on him, might have ridden into a mob war. If he had been killed . . . Andy could picture the astonishment and happiness in Miss Winnie's face when he told her, "Coley Joe wasn't a thief. He was a good, honorable man. He went with a friend into the wrong place at the wrong time and . . ."

But who was the friend?

Andy sighed. That was the number one question. He wished he knew.

As he drew near his house, a shadow seemed to rise from the bushes around his mailbox and leap into the even darker shadows under the oak trees.

Andy braked so fast that his bicycle wobbled. He jumped the curb, wheeled the bike into the grass, and leaped toward the shadows. "Hey!" he yelled. "Come out of there!"

No one answered. No one moved. Andy waited for an answer, but there was only silence.

CHAPTER ELEVEN

"You aren't going to get away from here!" Andy shouted into the darkness. "I'm not going to take my eyes off this spot, and I'm going to yell for the police. When they come . . ."

"Hey, Andy! Who are you talking to?" J.J. called from the driveway at the other side of Andy's house.

Andy took a step back and whirled around. "J.J.? What are you doing there?"

"I came to see you," J.J. said. He walked toward Andy. "I went to the back door, and your mom said you were at the library." As he joined Andy, he asked again, "Who were you talking to?"

Andy frowned. What if the shadow he'd seen had

been J.J.? He could have jumped into the darkness under the trees and kept going. It was possible that J.J. had circled around in back of the house.

"You, I think," Andy said.

"I don't mean now. I mean when I got here."

Andy looked into J.J.'s eyes. "I was just pulling up when I saw someone near our mailbox. I yelled at him, and he ran into the shadows under the trees. That's where I lost him."

J.J. looked into the shadows as if he were searching, too. "Weird," he said. "Who was it?"

"I don't know," Andy said. Expecting to find another warning, he strode over to the mailbox and opened it, but the mailbox was empty. "I think somebody was getting ready to deliver another warning letter," he told J.J. "Maybe I stopped him before he had a chance to leave it in the mailbox."

"Another warning?" J.J. asked. "A third one?"

"Yeah," Andy said. "Was that you I saw by the mailbox, J.J.?"

"Aw, c'mon, Andy," J.J. said. His glance slid away again, and he took another step backward.

"It was you, wasn't it?"

J.J.'s shoulders drooped as he shrugged and met Andy's eyes. "Okay. You were acting kind of strange when you left my house, so I thought I'd come over and see if you wanted to play a video game or something. Your mom said you were at the library, so I was going to leave, but I saw you coming. I thought it would be fun to jump out and scare you."

J.J. sighed. "But then you came running at me, yelling like you were mad and were going to fight. You scared me, Andy, so I cut around the house and came out the other way. That's all that happened. I haven't been sending you warning messages. We're best friends. Friends don't do things like that to each other."

When Andy didn't answer, J.J. walked past him and picked up his bike, which was lying next to the mailbox. "I'll see you around," he said.

Andy knew J.J. was right. They were best friends, and part of friendship was trust. He had to believe J.J. "Wait a minute," Andy said. "I was wrong and I'm sorry. I've been working so hard to find Coley Joe that I haven't been able to think about anything else."

J.J. hesitated. "Can I do something to help you find him?"

"Just tell me when I'm acting like a dope."

J.J. laughed, and Andy laughed, too.

"Did you finish going through Miss Winnie's box?" J.J. asked.

"No," Andy answered.

"Then why don't we do that now?" J.J. dropped his bike and helmet and came back to join Andy.

It was Andy's turn to hesitate. *J.J.'s my best friend*, he reminded himself. *I trust him. I have to.* "Okay. Thanks," Andy said.

They set up operations at the kitchen table, fortifying themselves with a stack of oatmeal cookies. Andy placed the bundles of sorted letters, bills of sale, children's drawings, and miscellaneous items in a row down one side of the table.

"Did you read all these letters?" J.J. asked.

Andy nodded. "Most of them are about business dealings. But there were some from Margaret Jane, who wrote home after she got married and moved to El Paso, and a couple were written by someone named Alice, who must have been Grace Elizabeth's sister."

"Did they say anything about Coley Joe?"

"Nothing."

For a few moments Andy and J.J. opened folded slips of paper, read them, and put them into the right piles.

Finally, J.J. said, "Most of this stuff is kind of boring."

Andy tucked a receipt into the right pile. "Yeah. At first I wondered why Malcolm John Bonner saved all these old tax receipts and bills of sale and stuff like that, but now I think I know why."

J.J. looked up. "Why?"

"Put all together they show how he kept buying land and cattle, how he built his ranch from almost nothing."

"That's something to be proud of," J.J. said, "no matter what Miz Minna says."

Andy leaned back in his chair. "How come Miz Minna knows so much about the Bonner family?"

J.J. shrugged. "Just nosy, I guess." His cheeks and nose grew pink as he said, "I told you, Miz Minna's a snob."

"She gave Miss Winnie a bad time, even when they were kids in school together," Andy said. "She must have known about Coley Joe and the lost money way back then."

J.J. laughed. "She knows about *everything*. And she keeps up with what's going on by asking a million questions."

For a moment Andy stopped breathing. "Like my search for Coley Joe? J.J., are you telling her everything I tell you?"

"Hey! Don't frown at me like that," J.J. said. "You're the one who asked Miz Minna if she knew anything about him."

"But that was before I figured out that she knew about the theft and had used the information to make Miss Winnie feel bad." He leaned forward and said, "J.J., promise me something. Promise me that you won't tell Miz Minna anything more about my search for Coley Joe."

"What more is there to tell?" J.J. asked. "Have you learned anything else about him?"

"I don't know yet. I won't know for a couple more

days. But there's a chance that Coley Joe was killed near El Paso. That means the money wasn't stolen by him. It might have been stolen by the person who killed him."

"Wow!" J.J. said. "Is this true?"

"I don't know. There are things I have to find out first."

"Andy! You're telling me that you're going to solve a mysterious disappearance—and maybe even a murder—over a hundred years old! You'll win that history contest Mr. Hammergren told you about!" He grinned. "When they take your picture for the newspaper, I'll stand next to you."

"Deal," Andy said.

"And after you find out, we'll keep your news a secret, right up to the big announcement," J.J. said. "It will knock Miz Minna right out of her boots."

"I hope," Andy said. "In the meantime don't tell her what I'm doing. I especially don't want Miz Minna to say anything about Coley Joe to Miss Winnie when she sees her at the Community Theatre tomorrow night. Miss Winnie doesn't know I'm still trying to get information about him."

"No problem," J.J. said. "They don't usually talk to each other. This time, if they look like they want to, we'll keep them apart. Now, c'mon. We've got all this stuff sorted. Let's put it back in the box and get to the video games."

Andy had planned on sleeping late on Saturday morning, but—like a recording—he heard Elton saying, "Find out what the Bonners have got to tell you."

Andy's own voice repeated, "Which Bonners?"

He awoke and sat up in bed. "Which Bonners?" he said aloud.

As he focused in on his alarm clock, he moaned. Only six-forty-five. Andy plunged back under the covers, pulling the pillow over his head. Coley Joe. He had to be the Bonner Elton had meant. Maybe on Monday afternoon, through Coley Joe, Andy would find the answer.

There was a tap on Andy's door, and it opened. "Hi," his dad said. "Unless you were just talking in your sleep, you're awake."

"Ummph," Andy mumbled.

"Good," Mr. Thomas said. "I'm making pancakes. After a big breakfast, how about helping me tackle the lawn and the shrubs? Your mother wants everything cut back and trimmed."

"Pancakes first?" Andy asked. "Is that a bribe?"

"Take it any way you want," his dad said, and laughed. "The agenda for the day doesn't change."

Andy heard his door shut, and he rolled over and climbed groggily out of bed. But by the time he was seated in front of a tall stack of his dad's pancakes, he was wide awake and hungry.

"I think the blue dress with the lace sleeves," his mother said as she came into the kitchen.

"Sounds good," his father answered.

"You said that about the red crepe dress."

Mr. Thomas smiled. "Can I help it if you look good in everything?"

Mrs. Thomas giggled before she bent to kiss the top of Andy's head. "Good morning, Andy," she said. "I know you've got soccer practice this afternoon, but be sure to be home in time for an early dinner and a bath. I'm picking up your suit at the cleaners and . . ."

"Mom!" Andy complained. "It's bad enough to have to go to the Community Theatre every time they put on a musical. But why do I have to wear a suit? Why can't I just be comfortable?"

"It's opening night, that's why."

"All the more reason why people should relax and be comfortable."

"I vote with Andy," Mr. Thomas said. He plopped a heaping pile of pancakes on his own plate and reached for the bottle of maple syrup. "Shorts and T-shirts. And no one has to shave or wear shoes if they don't want to."

"This conversation is impossible," Mrs. Thomas said. She waggled a finger at Andy. "Just remember what I told you about being home on time."

How could he forget? His mother reminded him at

lunch and again just before he set off for soccer practice. At the required time, Andy arrived home, took a bath, ate his dinner, and crammed himself into his shirt, tie, and suit.

"Hmmm," his mother said, "you're beginning to outgrow your suit already."

"I can wear something else," Andy said.

"No. This will do for tonight," Mrs. Thomas said. She looked at her watch. "The grandparents and Miss Winnie are coming with us," she said. "Let's get going."

Mr. Thomas dropped off his passengers at the front door of the theater. While he searched for a parking place, Andy and his grandfather helped Miss Winnie up the short ramp. As they reached the lobby of the Community Theatre, Andy glimpsed J.J. with his family. The top button of J.J.'s shirt was obviously too tight. J.J. looked as miserable as Andy.

Miz Minna, who had been talking to friends, turned to glance at Miss Winnie.

Quickly, Andy asked, "Miss Winnie, do you want me to help you to your seat?"

"Not yet, Andy boy," she said, and patted his shoulder. "I've got friends to greet."

She was soon surrounded, and Andy began to relax. It wasn't uncommon for Miz Minna to completely ignore Miss Winnie. He counted on her doing it again.

But next to his ear he heard Miz Minna's sugary voice rising, and he shuddered. She grabbed Andy's shoulder and leaned on it heavily, thrusting him forward.

"Winnie, I trust you are well," she said.

"Very well, and you?" Miss Winnie answered.

Miz Minna inclined her head and smiled. "Your clever grandnephew has been to visit me," she said.

Andy gulped and wished he could disappear.

J.J. squirmed and took Miz Minna's free hand. "I'll help you find our seats, Miz Minna," he said.

Andy threw J.J. a look of gratitude, but Miz Minna didn't budge.

"Andy seems bound and determined to dig up old family skeletons," Miz Minna continued. "However, I told him I'd never tell what I knew about the Bonners' family tragedy. He'd just have to ask you."

Miss Winnie's cheeks paled, but her eyes flashed angrily—first at Andy, then at Miz Minna. "I do appreciate the courtesy, Minna. It seems appropriate, considering that the Bonners' family history is none of anyone else's business."

Miz Minna didn't falter. "Oh, please don't blame the boy, Winnie. I'm sure he has no idea of how much pain he might cause by airing old family secrets."

Andy felt sick. That wasn't what he was trying to do at all. He was trying to prove that Coley Joe *hadn't* stolen the family's money. Didn't Miz Minna or Miss Winnie understand that?

"Now, if Andy were in *my* family, we could exercise

some control over his actions. I mean, if J.J., for instance, were told not to do something, he'd obey. Of course, nowadays so many children tend to be a little spoiled, a little uncaring about the wishes of others, and . . ."

Miss Winnie turned toward Grandpa. "Zeke," she said, "I do believe I'd like to take my seat now. The play will be starting soon."

"I'll help you, Miss Winnie," Andy said, but she ignored him and walked slowly away, leaning on Grandpa Zeke.

What Miz Minna had said about Andy had been just plain mean. *Why does she want to get me in trouble?* he wondered.

Andy trailed after his grandparents. He was glad his parents had been talking to friends and hadn't overheard the conversation.

But Grandma Dorothy turned as they reached the row of seats they'd purchased for the theater's season. Her expression was so sad that Andy cringed.

"I asked you, for Miss Winnie's sake, to forget about Coley Joe," she murmured.

"But I'm trying to prove Coley Joe didn't take the money," Andy explained.

Grandma Dorothy put a finger to her lips. "Miz Minna was right. You have no idea how much pain you have caused. Please, Andy, drop this foolish idea now, before you make the situation even worse."

Andy slunk into his seat and wished the play would begin so that this evening could soon be over. He was so close to an answer about Coley Joe. Too close to end the search. But the last thing he wanted to do was disobey his grandparents.

If he kept the rest of his search secret from anyone . . . If he . . .

Again Andy heard Elton's voice in his mind. "Find out what the Bonners have got to tell you."

Which Bonners? Who? Andy thought.

The warning gong sounded, people began hurrying to their seats, and the houselights dimmed.

There was no room for an answer.

CHAPTER TWELVE

A ndy couldn't concentrate on the musical. Over and over he thought of the information he had found and the questions that, so far, had no answers.

Coley Joe's friend had urged him to go to San Elizario.

In 1877 they didn't have TV or radio newscasts. And in fifth grade we learned, when we did that journalism study, that newspapers at that time were often weeklies, not dailies. Maybe the friend didn't know about the disturbance that was going on.

Then again, maybe he did.

Who was Coley Joe's El Paso friend?

Elton said he'd heard there was some kind of proof that had convinced Malcolm John that Coley Joe had stolen the money. And Grandma and Miz Minna talked about proof. What was this so-called proof? If no one knew what it was, how were they sure it was right? If—

His mother's voice broke into Andy's thoughts. "It's intermission time. Don't you want to get up and stretch?"

Andy saw J.J. signaling him from the side aisle, so he jumped up. "Sure," he said, and cut across an empty row of seats to reach J.J.

"I'm sorry about Miz Minna," J.J. said. "I didn't know she'd double-cross you like that."

"Why'd she do it?" Andy asked.

"I think she's jealous that you got into the genealogy bulletin boards," J.J. said. "She thinks that's her own private property, since she did so much research on her family through the boards."

"But she told me about the boards."

"I know." J.J. glanced toward his family. "If it helps you feel any better, Miz Minna gives my mom a bad time, too. The older she gets, the crankier she gets."

"I'm scared that after Mom and Dad talk to Grandma and find out what happened tonight, they'll tell me I can't keep on with my search for Coley Joe."

J.J. nodded sympathetically. "Are you sure you really want to?" he asked. "You haven't found any real proof that he *wasn't* a thief."

"But I'm getting closer, J.J.," Andy said. "I can't stop now."

The houselights dimmed and rose again, the signal to the members of the audience to return to their seats.

"Remember, I told you I'd share with you whatever information I got from Miz Minna," J.J. said. "I'll bring it over tomorrow if you like."

Andy shook his head. "Thanks, but I don't need it. Miss Winnie and Grandpa and Grandma told me all sorts of stuff about what life was like when they were young. It's plenty for my history report."

"Okay," J.J. said, "but this goes back to January of 1878, when the first James Jonathan Gasper came from El Paso to Hermosa."

"Thanks, anyway," Andy said, "but the only person I'm interested in around that time is Coley Joe Bonner."

"Whatever," J.J. said. "If you change your mind, just let me know."

After church the next morning, Andy's parents sat with him in the den, and his mom recounted what Grandma Dorothy had told her about Miz Minna's conversation with Miss Winnie at the theater.

"Miz Minna said all that stuff to be mean," Andy grumbled.

"That's beside the point. I understand Miss Winnie had asked you to forget about Coley Joe," Mrs. Thomas said.

119

Andy leaned forward. "That's right, Mom. She said I shouldn't ask her questions because she wouldn't answer them. But she didn't actually tell me I couldn't investigate."

Mr. Thomas looked serious. "Well, now it's time to lay down a rule. In the future . . ."

"Dad! Wait!" Andy begged. "Let me tell you what I'm doing." His mind raced frantically through the adolescent psychology book until he reached the words that would get the right reaction from his parents. "I need to know that you respect what I have to say and that you trust me."

His mother threw a look at his father. "Well, of course we do, Andy. We're here to listen. We certainly want to hear what you have to say."

"Okay," Andy said. He took a deep breath and began. "All these years later Miss Winnie's upset about some ancestor she didn't even know who was supposed to have stolen money from his family—"

Mr. Thomas interrupted. "It's true she's taken the theft to heart, but think about it. Because the money was stolen, the family suffered great hardships. Because the money was stolen, Miss Winnie's had to live with the fact that one of her relatives was a particularly nasty crook, robbing his own parents."

"And be reminded of it now and again by Miz Minna," Mrs. Thomas added. "Unfortunately, your family search has brought the story to life again. Last night was humiliating for Miss Winnie."

"I'm sorry," Andy said. "I didn't know that was going to happen."

"So therefore—" his father began.

"I haven't finished!" Andy was desperate. "You said you'd listen to me."

Mr. Thomas looked at his watch. "Make it quick," he said.

"I don't believe Coley Joe took the money," Andy told them. He told them all he had learned about Coley Joe, then added, "And tomorrow Mrs. Alonzo may find out if there's any record that Coley Joe was killed at San Elizario."

Mrs. Thomas's eyes sparkled. "Andy, that's a wonderful piece of research. And Mr. Hammergren thinks you can enter a contest and maybe win a scholarship for it? How exciting!"

Mr. Thomas rubbed his chin. "If Andy can prove his case, think what that will mean to Miss Winnie."

"Does that mean you'll let me keep on searching?" Andy asked.

"Well . . ." Mrs. Thomas glanced toward the house next door. "Both Miss Winnie and Grandma Dorothy asked us to forbid you to even mention Coley Joe again."

"Suppose we reach a compromise," Mr. Thomas

said. "You said you might find out tomorrow if Coley Joe was listed among those who were killed at San Elizario?"

Andy nodded.

"We'll give you a few more days," Mr. Thomas told Andy. "You should know by then if you're making any progress or if you've come to a dead end."

"What about the scholarship contest?"

"You can't very well write an essay about your search if you haven't turned up anything conclusive, can you?"

"I know what you mean."

"I see a couple of real problems, unless you've found information you haven't mentioned to us," Mr. Thomas said. "Elton told you that the Bonners had proof that Coley Joe was the thief. Miz Minna and even Grandma said something about proof. What is this proof?"

"I don't know yet," Andy said. "I don't think they do either."

"You have to face the fact that this *proof,* if you find it, may make all your work come to nothing."

His mother put a hand on Andy's shoulder and smiled. "Don't look so discouraged, Andy. We're proud of what you've done. You gave yourself a goal, and you're doing your best to reach it. That's what's important, not whether Coley Joe Bonner is guilty or innocent."

But Andy didn't agree. Proving Coley Joe innocent

122

was what he had started out to do, and he wouldn't be satisfied until he'd accomplished it.

That afternoon, when J.J. came over, he brought a sheaf of papers. "You said you didn't need these, but I thought you might change your mind," he said. He pointed to the top sheet. "It all starts in January 1878, with the first James Jonathan Gasper, when he came to Hermosa and invested in a mercantile company and a bank. That's where he made his big start."

Andy glanced at the papers, then tossed them onto the table. At the moment, the last thing he was interested in was the history of the Gasper family. "Thanks," he said to J.J. "Want to ride down to the park and see if anyone's got a basketball game going?"

"Sure," J.J. answered. "Anything but homework."

On Monday, Andy couldn't keep his mind on his classwork. All he could think about was what Mrs. Alonzo might find out about Coley Joe.

History class ended, with Mr. Hammergren's reminder that the family reports were due on Friday. But as Andy followed J.J., heading toward the door, Mr. Hammergren stopped him.

"What's up, Andy?" he asked. "You've been jumpy as a pup with chiggers."

"Mrs. Alonzo, down at the library, said she'd contact the Texas State Archives in Austin. She said there were probably official reports about the Salt Wars, and they might contain the names of the four men who were killed there."

"And you're hoping that one of them was Coley Joe Bonner."

"It's worth a try."

Mr. Hammergren smiled and held up a sheet of paper. "Here are the rules for entering that state history contest I told you about. I asked the head of the committee to fax them to me."

"I told my mom and dad about the contest," Andy said. "My mom got kind of excited."

Mr. Hammergren grinned. "I'm excited, too. Let me know what you find out today. Okay?"

"You bet I will," Andy said. He ran to catch up with J.J.

After school Andy pedaled to the library as fast as he could, grumbling at stoplights and slow-moving pickup trucks. He leaped from his bike, shoved it into the parking rack, and raced up the steps of the James Jonathan Gasper Memorial Library.

As Andy skidded to a stop at the check-in desk, Mrs. Alonzo looked up and smiled.

"Come with me," she said. "I've got some information for you."

"About Coley Joe?" Andy asked. His stomach knotted, and it was hard to breathe.

Mrs. Alonzo didn't answer. She sat with Andy at a table in the far corner and spread out two sheets of paper. "Here's the name of the woman I talked to in the Texas State Archives office. She said they are allowed to spend up to forty minutes on each telephoned question, and no more, but she was able to give me the information I asked for."

"About Coley Joe?" Andy repeated.

Mrs. Alonzo couldn't be hurried. "There are two reports in the archives," she said. "One is 'The Adjutant General's Report for the Fiscal Year,' published on August 1, 1878. The other is Executive Document number 93, from the Forty-fifth Congress, second session, Texas House of Representatives, titled, 'El Paso Troubles in Texas.' The first is the U.S. Army's official report, which includes the Salt Wars. The second contains the report of the Texas Rangers."

Andy couldn't stand the suspense. "Do they say anything about Coley Joe?"

Mrs. Alonzo sighed. "Not exactly," she said.

"Not exactly? What does that mean?"

"It means that those four men who were killed—the men mentioned in *The Handbook of Texas*—are identified and named in the reports. None of them was Coley Joe Bonner."

Andy slid down in his chair and scowled at his toes. "I was hoping so hard I'd find him," he mumbled.

"Don't give up," Mrs. Alonzo told him. "These were men known in the community. The Texas Rangers' report goes on to mention numerous murders and robberies."

"Murders?"

"There's a description of the mob action in looting and various shootings. Some looters were killed, and some ran off into Mexico to escape the law."

"Coley Joe wasn't part of a mob. He wouldn't loot."

"Of course he wouldn't. But if his body was found in the area of the riots and he had no identification, he could have been mistaken for someone in the mob of rioters."

"Hey! Yeah!" Andy said. He slid back up in his chair, hope rising again until he realized that more than a hundred years later there'd be no way of identifying Coley Joe.

"Did Coley Joe Bonner have any unusual identifying marks that might have attracted notice?" Mrs. Alonzo asked.

Andy shrugged. "You mean like a birthmark or . . ." He sat upright. "A nail!" he said. "Each of the men in the Bonner family wore a nail, hammered into a circle, on a leather thong around his neck.

126

Like . . ." He reached for the one he had worn briefly, suddenly remembering that it was still lying on top of Grace Elizabeth's poetry book in his bedroom.

"The reports didn't go into details like that," Mrs. Alonzo said. "But there are other places we can try."

Andy was puzzled. "Like what?"

"Think about it. Where do you get detailed information when local crimes are committed?"

"TV news!"

"In 1877?"

Andy laughed. "Okay, in newspapers."

"Surely El Paso was large enough to have a newspaper in 1877. Let's find out."

"How?" Andy asked.

Mrs. Alonzo shoved back her chair and beckoned to Andy. "We'll call the Texas History Department at the El Paso Public Library."

Andy waited by the counter near her desk while Mrs. Alonzo made the telephone call. At one point she covered the mouthpiece of the phone with her hand and said, "There was a semiweekly newspaper called *The Lone Star,* published from 1876 through 1888. They have only scattered copies—among them very few in the seventies—but she's going to see what might turn up."

Mrs. Alonzo suddenly turned back to the phone. "No description of the bodies? I see. Who?" She picked up a pen and began writing. Finally she thanked whomever she was talking to and hung up the phone. She handed Andy a slip of paper.

"There's a history professor at the University of Texas at El Paso who's a collector. He owns a few early copies of *The Lone Star* that might have the information you need."

Andy read the name: Dr. Palius Rundle.

Could Dr. Palius Rundle be DrPR? The person he'd met through e-mail? All this time, had DrPR held the answer?

CHAPTER THIRTEEN

As he pedaled for home, Andy realized with embarrassment that he had never thanked DrPR for his earlier information. Well, now he'd thank him and ask him for new information—all at the same time.

In spite of his trip to the library, Andy was still the first one home. Not even stopping for something to eat, he booted up the computer and clicked on *e-mail*. The message from DrPR was still there, so Andy clicked on *reply,* and a fresh writing screen came up.

"Thanks for the information about *The Handbook of Texas,*" Andy wrote. He went on to tell DrPR about his guess that Coley Joe might have been killed in San Elizario. "He was probably medium tall," Andy wrote, "with dark, curly hair. He may have died without any identification, but he wore a horseshoe nail, hammered into a circle, on a leather thong around his neck. It wasn't valuable to anyone except the men in the Bonner family, so it wasn't likely to have been stolen. If you can find a news story in your collector's copies of *The Lone Star* that describes any of the unidentified victims found after the battle, I would really appreciate hearing from you by e-mail." He thought a moment and added, "as soon as possible." Then he ended with "Thank you."

Before sending the message, Andy hesitated. He jumped out of the chair, raced upstairs, and grabbed the hammered nail, pulling the thong over his head. Without a pause, he galloped down the stairs into his dad's office and clicked on *send.* It wasn't that he was superstitious or anything like that. He, Andy, was a Bonner and related to Coley Joe. He would wear the Bonner nail until he closed the circle by proving that Coley Joe was not a thief.

He reached out to disconnect the modem when the computer's voice announced, "You've got mail."

Andy clicked on the mailbox icon, holding his breath as he saw that there was an e-mail message for him from DrPR. He pressed *enter,* and up came a letter.

"You know about my collection, Hunter, so you must know my name. How did you find out?"

Andy wrote back, "Through the Texas History Department of the El Paso Public Library. They gave my librarian your name and address. I'm the one who made the e-mail connection. I didn't write to you by snail mail, because if I don't come up with the answers this week, my dad says I have to stop my search. Do you want to know more about Coley Joe?"

The answer arrived less than a minute after Andy had sent his message. "I'm very much interested. And I'm interested in you and why you're researching this person."

Andy told DrPR about Coley Joe and how everyone had believed that he'd stolen his parents' money and disgraced his family. He told him that Coley Joe had written to his girlfriend that he was going to San Elizario to buy cattle from someone who was eager to sell. Then he wrote that he, Hunter, was in the seventh grade and all this had started with a homework assignment to interview older family members about their lifestyles when they were young.

The answer Andy had hoped for came back. "Here's something I found in a December 1877 issue of *The Lone Star*. This might be the information for which you're searching."

DrPR went on to copy part of a newspaper article:

THE STREETS WERE SHOWERED WITH BROKEN GLASS AND
SPLINTERED WOOD, WRECKAGE LEFT BY THE MOB THAT
LOOTED SAN ELIZARIO, THEN FLED TO MEXICO TO
ESCAPE THE POSSE COMPOSED OF ANGRY CITIZENS,
TEXAS RANGERS, AND UNITED STATES ARMY TROOPS.

HERE AND THERE WERE SCATTERED THE LIFELESS FORMS OF THE FEW WHO HAD BEEN CUT DOWN BY GUNFIRE BEFORE THEY COULD ESCAPE. ONE HAD BEEN A BOY, PROBABLY ONLY FOURTEEN OR FIFTEEN YEARS OF AGE WHEN HE DIED, HIS POCKETS FILLED WITH STOLEN ITEMS. NEAR WHERE I STOOD LAY THE BODY OF A DARK-HAIRED YOUNG MAN WHO HAD BEEN SHOT IN THE BACK OF THE HEAD. HIS SHIRT AND JACKET WERE MISSING, HIS TROUSERS TORN, AND AROUND HIS NECK, ON A LEATHER THONG, HE WORE AN INEXPENSIVE HORSESHOE NAIL, HAMMERED INTO A CIRCLE.

Andy let out a yelp and jumped up so fast, his chair toppled over. "It was Coley Joe!" he shouted. "I found Coley Joe!"

But as Andy thought again about what he had read, he pictured Coley Joe lying dead among strangers, no one even knowing who he was. With a sorrow that made his eyes burn and his throat ache, Andy righted the chair and lowered himself into it. "I'm sorry, Coley Joe," he said aloud. "But all along I knew you hadn't taken the money. This news story proves it. Now maybe everyone will believe me."

Andy printed the letter, then sent an e-mail message to thank DrPR.

"It was a pleasure to help you in your quest," DrPR replied. "I hope we may correspond again."

Andy exited Windows and turned off the computer.

So excited that his heart was thumping in his ears, he climbed the stairs to his bedroom.

Scarcely realizing what he was doing, he sat on the edge of his bed and picked up the poetry book. In his mind rose the vision of the sad-eyed woman who had looked at him so beseechingly in his dream. He felt as if he were back in the dream, gray mists swimming around him. "Miz Grace Elizabeth, your son didn't steal your money," Andy murmured aloud.

The telephone suddenly rang, whamming Andy into the present. He started so violently that the book sailed from his hands, slamming against his chest of drawers.

Andy ran into his parents' room and caught the phone on its third ring.

"Andy dear." Miz Minna's voice purred in his ear.

Andy grimaced. The last person in the world he wanted to talk to was Miz Minna. "I'm sorry," he said politely, "J.J.'s not here."

"Oh, I know that," Miz Minna said. "I don't want to talk with J.J. He's gone shoe shopping with his mama and won't be back for a couple of hours. It's you I want to talk to—while J.J.'s not here."

"Miz Minna, ma'am, I don't think I—"

Her voice sharpened. "Andy, we need to talk. I'd very much appreciate it if you'd come on over here within the next fifteen or twenty minutes. Lila will let you in."

As Andy paused, she said, "I told you about proof

133

that Coley Joe stole his family's money. Well, I've got that proof, and now I'm willing to show it to you."

Andy thought about the information he'd received from Dr. Palius Rundle. "I don't need to see it," Andy said.

Miz Minna sighed and said, "My, my, you're a stubborn boy. Well, here's one warning you just might pay attention to. You get over here and see what I've got to show you, or I'll send a copy of it directly to Miss Winnie. Maybe even to the newspapers."

Andy frowned at the phone. Miz Minna had no right to hurt Miss Winnie. And he knew that Miz Minna had no real proof that Coley Joe was a thief. She was either mistaken or lying to him. But Andy's curiosity was growing. The least he could do was see what she insisted on showing him.

He walked slowly back to his room and bent to pick up the poetry book. Its front cover was twisted back, the endpaper pulled away from the binding, exposing dried splotches of glue.

As Andy gently picked up the book, he saw two thin, folded sheets of paper that had been tucked underneath the endpaper.

They were brittle, and they crackled as he carefully smoothed them out to read them. As he recognized the handwriting on the first letter, Andy sucked in his breath.

Dearest Mother, the letter began. As in the letters

Coley Joe had written to Felicity, he described the thriving town of El Paso, with its heat and bustling traffic that kicked up clouds of choking dust on its dry streets. He even spoke about its background of purple-shadowed mountains, whose rugged peaks stretched into a clear, cloudless sky.

Then he wrote:

I treasure the trust that you and Father have placed in me by allowing me to purchase livestock and make arrangements for the building of our new home. My friend, James Jonathan Gasper, chief clerk for District Judge Charles Howard, will accompany me to San Elizario to buy cattle.

Coley Joe had written loving messages to the rest of his family, but Andy was unable to read them. Stunned by his discovery, he sat with the letter on his lap, staring into space. What had J.J.'s information sheet said about the first James Jonathan Gasper? He had come to Hermosa in January 1878. That was one month after Coley Joe's death.

And J.J. the First had come to Hermosa with enough money to open a mercantile store and found a bank, even though Coley Joe had written to Felicity that his friend had little money and was underpaid.

With trembling fingers Andy picked up the second letter. It was written in a bolder hand than Coley Joe's,

and the signature at the bottom was that of James Jonathan Gasper.

Dated March 1878, the letter began:

*How fortunate that your son had given you my name,
so that you were able to trace my whereabouts to Hermosa. I am unable to satisfactorily answer all your
inquiries, however. Cole Joseph Bonner and I were not
friends. We were mere acquaintances, so I was unaware
of his obligations to his family and that he had broken
off communication with you.*

*I don't understand why he told you that I'd be ac-
companying him to San Elizario. It pains me to inform
you that the information he gave you was false. In truth,
on the twentieth of last December I met Cole Joseph on
the street outside my boarding house as he was preparing
to ride west. As he had mentioned earlier, on at least
two occasions, he saw his future not in Texas, but in
California. He was planning to travel with a young
woman whose name I do not know.*

Andy folded the letters again and tucked them into
the poetry book.

Coley Joe had been shot and killed. His identification and his family's money had been stolen, and a terrible lie had been told about him—a lie that would keep
Felicity, as well as his parents, from hunting for him.

What am I going to do? Andy wondered. His search
for Coley Joe had turned up the truth, as he had hoped.

But the truth meant that Andy's best friend's great-great-great-great-grandfather—a founding father and leading citizen in Hermosa—had been a liar, a thief, and a murderer!

CHAPTER FOURTEEN

Andy was still shaky when he arrived at the Gasper house. Although Mrs. Martinez tried to tease him as she led him to Miz Minna's room, he couldn't even manage a smile.

"Don't be scared of Miz Minna," Mrs. Martinez whispered. "She rarely bites."

Andy didn't try to explain. He just shook his head and followed Lila Martinez into Miz Minna's room.

"How about a Coke? And brownies?" Mrs. Martinez asked Andy.

"No thanks," Andy said. "I'm not hungry." He pressed a hand against his stomach, which ached the way it had when he'd come down with the flu.

Miz Minna was seated in her big armchair, pearls draped in two long rows across her chest, a faded cloth-covered book in her hands. She bowed her head toward Andy as though she were queen and he had come to ask a favor.

"Sit down over there, Andy," she said in a voice as warm as honey. "Be careful of the flowers. Don't tump over that vase."

"Yes, ma'am," Andy said.

As Mrs. Martinez left, Miz Minna held up the book so that Andy could see it. He reached for it, but she snatched it back. "I told you I had the first James Jonathan Gasper's journal. Remember?"

"Yes," Andy said.

"And I told you I had proof that your Coley Joe Bonner was a thief."

"No, Miz Minna. You don't."

"What do you mean, I don't?" Her eyes darkened, and her gaze flickered across Andy's face. "I do, indeed, have proof, and I'm going to read it to you right now."

Miz Minna opened the journal to a page marked with a bookmark and read aloud, " 'Coley Joe Bonner's parents contacted me by mail and asked if I knew the whereabouts of their son. It took me by surprise. I didn't know he had given them my name. There was nothing to do but inform them that their son had headed west to seek his fortune in California.' "

She closed the book and smiled triumphantly. "There you have it," she said. "The words are in his own handwriting."

Andy stared into Miz Minna's eyes. "You don't believe what he wrote, either," he said. "That's why the warnings. You're the one who's been threatening me."

Miz Minna gasped, her hands flying to her throat. "What are you talking about? What warnings? What threats?"

"Until a little while ago I didn't know who wanted to stop me from finding out the truth about Coley Joe, or why it would be important to anyone." Andy sighed. "I even wondered once if it might be J.J., because the warnings had to do with things I'd told only him. But you knew, too. You asked J.J. what I was discovering, and he trusted you. He told you."

"This is ridiculous," Miz Minna said.

"When you telephoned me half an hour ago, you said that this was one warning I'd pay attention to. So you knew about the others. You sent me the others."

She smoothed down her skirt with nervous fingers and picked up a small brass bell. "You'd better leave. I'll ring for Lila."

"Miz Minna," Andy said. "I have proof, too. Mine comes from a newspaper called *The Lone Star*. In an article in the paper that told what San Elizario was like after the last battle of the Salt Wars, the reporter described the body of Coley Joe. He'd been shot in the back of the head. His money, his ID, his shirt, and his coat had all been stolen. But the murderer had left

140

something he didn't know was valuable. He'd left the Bonner circle around Coley Joe's neck."

Andy pulled his own circle from inside his shirt and held it out so that Miz Minna could see it.

She stared, not at the circular nail, but at Andy, her face so pale that little spots of pink rouge on her cheeks stood out like a rash.

"For many years, since you and Miss Winnie were kids, you made her unhappy by telling her what you just read to me," Andy said. "But I think that when you got so interested in the genealogy of your family and started adding things up, you realized the famous James Jonathan Gasper the First was a liar, a thief, and a murderer. Then when I began searching for information about Coley Joe, you got scared that I'd find out, too, and Miss Winnie and the rest of Hermosa would know the truth."

Miz Minna cried out, "How can you say such a horrible thing?"

"Because it's true, Miz Minna," Andy said. "The first J.J. was a clerk, in a low-paying job. How did he suddenly come into enough money to move to Hermosa and establish both a store and a bank?"

"I–I . . . there are many ways of acquiring investment money."

"Coley Joe didn't ride west. Coley Joe was murdered in San Elizario by the first James Jonathan Gasper. The newspaper article, along with some letters, proves it."

"What letters?"

"Two letters his mother had hidden and saved. One was written by Coley Joe and names James Jonathan Gasper as the friend who was leading him to San Elizario. The other letter was the terrible lie James Jonathan wrote."

Miz Minna shrunk back and gripped the arms of the chair with bloodless fingers. "If you write the story for that contest J.J. told me about, you'll destroy our entire family. You'll destroy James Jonathan Gasper's memory."

"I know," Andy said. "Believe me, on the way over here I thought hard about that." He clasped his hands, staring down at them for a few moments before he looked up at Miz Minna. "But knowing the truth will make Miss Winnie feel an awful lot better. And if I win the statewide essay contest, it will make my parents real proud."

"The Gasper name has long been honorable."

"There's nothing honorable about murder," Andy answered. "And there's nothing honorable about what you did. You knew that your family had cheated the Bonner family out of a large sum of money, and you hid the information."

"I beg you, don't write the essay," Miz Minna pleaded.

"Please don't say that, Miz Minna." Andy squirmed

142

uncomfortably. "You don't have to beg. I'm going to do what I think is right, and you ought to think about doing what's right, too."

"Which is?"

"I'm not sure yet," Andy answered. "There's a lot of people involved in this story. Some of them are going to have to give up something. Others are going to come out ahead. I don't want to hurt anybody, Miz Minna. Trust me. There's been too much hurt already."

Andy felt a little sick as he walked away from Miz Minna. She had shrunken into a pitiful old lady who looked at least a hundred years old. He let himself out of the house, climbed on his bike, and fastened his helmet.

"Find out what the Bonners have got to tell you," Elton Gillie had said. Well, maybe now it was time to ask another question of a Bonner who had given him answers: Grace Elizabeth, Coley Joe's mother.

It didn't take long to pedal out of town and onto the highway that led to the cemetery. The gate stood open, although there was no sign of Elton.

The tombstones cast late-afternoon shadows, and the silence was broken only by soft rustles and snips among the long grass.

Andy easily found Malcolm John Bonner's dark red stone. Next to it was a smaller, modest stone in yellow sandstone, with the name Grace Elizabeth Bonner, the dates of her birth and death—twelve years before her husband's—and the inscription "devoted wife and mother."

"Miz Grace Elizabeth, I got your letters," Andy said. "And I've got the proof that Coley Joe was murdered in San Elizario. I even know the name of the murderer."

As he said the words, a burst of excitement shot through his body like bubbles from a Coke that had been given a good shaking up. "Hey, did you hear that?" he shouted. "I solved a murder that took place around a hundred and twenty years ago! I really did!"

Andy could picture Miss Winnie's rejoicing, Mom's and Dad's happy praise, Mr. Hammergren's big grin. Andy saw himself beaming at the television cameras— J.J. at his side—as he said, "I'm happy to accept this Texas State History Award because I . . ."

J.J. at his side.

Soberly, he turned his thoughts back to Grace Elizabeth. "I've got a problem, ma'am," he said. "You see, J.J. Gasper the Seventh is my best friend. I wouldn't want to do anything that would hurt my best friend."

Andy sat on a nearby tombstone and leaned forward, turning his bicycle helmet around and around in his hands. "I know you'd want your son's name cleared. Any mother would. And I can do that if I tell Miss Winnie only up to the part where Coley Joe was shot in San Elizario. He didn't run off with his family's money.

He wasn't a thief. He was caught in a mob and shot and robbed. That's all Miss Winnie needs to know. That's enough to bring Coley Joe out of the shadows. Miss Winnie won't think of asking who did it, because she won't believe anyone could find out. So she'll be satisfied."

Andy cleared his throat before he could speak again. "It's kind of embarrassing to say, ma'am, but Miss Winnie's the only one any more who really suffers that much about the so-called family scandal. I mean, Grandma and Grandpa worry about how Miss Winnie feels, but they aren't upset about what Coley Joe did or didn't do. And I don't think my parents mind one way or the other."

The cemetery seemed even more silent than before until a bee buzzed through the sprigs of clover and sailed lazily on.

"I'm trying to say that if I write about Coley Joe's murder, I can't give any clues as to who did it. I can't put in finding out anything about the first James Jonathan Gasper, because somebody else might start figuring things out. I even have to leave out parts of the letters to you and to Felicity, so it may not be much of a report when I get right down to it. So I'm asking, Is that okay with you?"

From the corners of his eyes Andy saw Elton Gillie approaching, lumbering up the rise like a short, fat bear.

"Hey, there," Elton said, as he came near. "You still tryin' to get answers from the Bonners?"

"Yeah, I guess," Andy said.

"And not doin' too good this time. I can tell from your face." Elton chuckled. "Remember, I told you, the dead can slip you an idea or two, but there are some things, like the big answers, you got to figure out for yourself."

The big answers. Of course. Those big answers belonged to Andy, and he was sure now what he was going to do.

He stood up and grinned. His worries had disappeared so fast, he was light-headed. If Elton hadn't been standing right in front of him, Andy would have jumped around and yelled and laughed like a maniac.

"I found out what I wanted, so I'm going along home," Andy said to Elton. "I've got something real important to tell my great-aunt Winnie, and it won't wait."

One Thing Leads to
Another ... and Another

As he had planned, Andy told Miss Winnie only the part of the story that had to do with Coley Joe's death and the robbery that had followed. Miss Winnie shed buckets of tears for poor Coley Joe, whose memory had been so unfairly tarnished. Then she cried for happiness that finally the truth had been made known.

Grandma Dorothy made Andy his favorite chocolate cake, and Grandpa Zeke bought him a real pro basketball. For two days Andy was king in his household. But celebrations don't last forever, so he soon found himself once again taking out the trash, doing the dinner dishes, and raking leaves.

Andy entered the statewide history essay contest by writing about his search for Coley Joe, leaving out anything that could possibly lead back to the first James

Jonathan Gasper. His story ended with Coley Joe, on his way to buy cattle, being surrounded, robbed, and killed as the mob of looters escaped into Mexico.

Mr. Hammergren gave Andy an A on the essay, an A on his family's oral history report, and an A on his report card. Andy's essay didn't win the first-place scholarship in the contest, but after Mr. Hammergren told the news director of the local television station about Andy's project, the news crew came out to the school and videotaped him anyway.

J.J., as Andy's best friend and agent, stood proudly at his side.

Miz Minna hosted an elegant tea party, at which Miss Winnie was guest of honor. Miz Minna announced that she had established a foundation honoring Cole Joseph Bonner. The purpose of the foundation would be to provide full college scholarships to worthy students in Hermosa. The first recipient would be Andrew Thomas.

The topic of conversation *after* the party was not the very large amount of money Miz Minna had put into the foundation. It was Miz Minna's gracious behavior. Not even the eldest of the elderly women in Hermosa's social circle could ever remember Miz Minna's being so well behaved.

Andy reframed the old Bonner family photograph, this time with Coley Joe in it. He bought a small metal strongbox, locked away the letters that would have incriminated James Jonathan Gasper, and hid the box at the bottom of his closet behind his sweaty gym shoes and socks, where it would be safe for a million years.

And Andy, proud of being a Bonner through his father's side of the family, wore around his neck, night and day, the leather thong with the Bonner family's circle.

AUTHOR'S NOTE

Texas, the Lone Star State, is large enough to fit fifteen of our fifty states inside its borders and have a thousand square miles left over. It is said that Texas folk hero Pecos Bill used a hurricane to fan himself. At one time Texas was an independent nation, the Republic of Texas. The republic's flag, with its Lone Star, remains the state flag today. Texas joined the Union as the twenty-eighth state in 1845.

With its many lakes and streams, Texas is second only to Alaska in volume of inland water, but it has vast stretches of desert land. It's made up of mountains and minerals, caverns and canyons, seashore and seashells, farms and forests, museums and monuments, bougain-villeas and bluebonnets, cowboys and cattle, ranches and rattlesnakes, prairies and petroleum, cities and country stores, and sunshine and swamps. Texas has dinosaur bones to recall the past and wildlife refuges to protect the future. And it's the site of NASA and the magnifi-cent Johnson Space Center, in Houston.

The battle at the Alamo and the Battle of San Jacinto are two of the most famous Texas battles for freedom and independence. But there were other, lesser-known battles, fought to preserve what was right. One of these, in 1877, was the Texas Salt Wars. *Search for the Shadowman* explores this unique and exciting period of Texas history.

Joan Lowery Nixon